P9-BYR-332

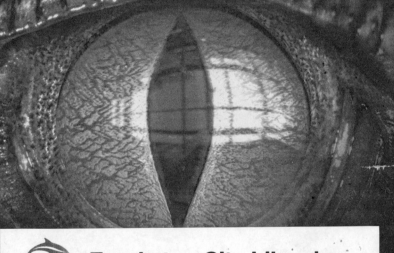

From the Chicken House

I took my children to a factory farm once, by mistake really (it was run by a neighbour). There were lines and lines of pigs, all in tiny cages. The boys were shouting about sausages and pies, and the girls were sobbing and pledging themselves to a life of vegetarianism.

I'd never *really* thought about where food comes from – and where *we* are in the food chain! Now M. J. Howes *really* puts us in the picture . . . and I have definitely, finally gone off hamburgers – for ever.

Barry Cunningham
Publisher

FEED

M.J.HOWES

Chicken House

2 Palmer Street, Frome, Somerset BA11 1DS
www.doublecluck.com.

Text © M. J. Howes 2014
First published in Great Britain in 2014
The Chicken House
2 Palmer Street
Frome, Somerset, BA11 1DS
United Kingdom
www.doublecluck.com

M. J. Howes has asserted her right under the Copyright, Designs and Patents Act 1988,
to be identified as the author of this work.

Cover design and interior design by Steve Wells
Typeset by Dorchester Typesetting Group Ltd
Printed and bound in Great Britain by CPI Group (UK) Ltd, Croydon, CR0 4YY
The paper used in this Chicken House book is made from wood
grown in sustainable forests.

1 3 5 7 9 10 8 6 4 2

British Library Cataloguing in Publication data available.

ISBN 978-1-908435-96-5

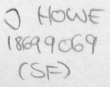
J HOWE
18699069
(SF)

Pippa and Alex
— for just being you, don't ever change

Chapter One

The calm before the storm. That's how I see every day now. Just waiting for the next raid. Wondering who'll be taken next.

I lean back on the rail of the squeaky old roundabout. Patrick sits next to me, turning it gently with his foot, kicking up chips of bark.

'Had the nightmare last night,' he says, casually, like it's normal.

'Well, I haven't had it for a week. Maybe I should get some kind of medal.' I laugh, but it's a hollow sound. 'Was it bad?'

'Yeah, I was sick after.'

'I'm sorry,' I say, linking my little finger around his, a silly gesture we've done since primary school.

No one can explain the identical nightmare we all share. The putrid stench that chokes us in our sleep. The rasping and squelching in the darkness. The jaws descending. The moment our bodies are ripped apart. And the terrifying screams that wake us.

Without warning, Patrick digs his heel into the ground. I lurch forwards, the roundabout juddering to a stop.

'What was that?' He's pointing to the sky.

'What?' My pulse quickens. 'I . . . I don't see anything.'

Musket, my black Labrador, gets to his feet, ears pricked, ready for anything.

'There was something above the trees. Did you see it?'

I frantically scan the treetops; there's a white, flapping thing caught in the gnarled fingers of an oak.

'It's . . . it looks like a plastic bag.'

Patrick breathes out. 'I'm freaking out over a stupid bag,' he mumbles, looking at the floor. 'I should've gone back to school this afternoon instead of bunking off – maybe I'd've learned how not to be an idiot.'

'It's okay,' I say, touching his arm.

'No, it's not,' he sighs. 'I'm losing it, Lola. Big time.'

'Don't say that,' I snap. 'Don't ever say that . . . And anyway, would you really rather be at school doing algebra or hanging out here, being an idiot?'

He looks up, his smile back. 'Algebra? Oh yeah, totally. You know me.'

We both laugh. This is the one place we can still be ourselves. We feel safe here, surrounded by the trees and the broken swings and slides of the playground. It's our haven.

'Anyway, you don't need to go to school,' I say. 'You know everything there is to know already.'

'Well, I can't help it if I'm a genius,' he grins.

I think about our school and the few students who still go every day – but only because their parents make them. Like my mum does. Trying to pretend life is normal. I stare down at my school uniform – black blazer, black trousers, white shirt and red striped tie. I used to think it looked smart. Now it looks all wrong. Everything looks wrong.

Patrick spins us again. I close my eyes and throw back my head. I love the feeling – the jumbled sense of direction, the cold air against my cheeks. I could be anywhere right now. Riding the waves in a speed boat or skydiving through the clouds. Anywhere but here . . .

Then reality bites back. Our reality.

Sirens.

The air, our senses, every living thing is engulfed by the same familiar, torturing sound. The sound of our nights for the past three years.

Patrick stops the roundabout dead. We stare at each other.

'A raid,' he mouths, his expression as confused and terrified as my own must be.

'Can't be, it's still daylight.'

'Yeah, and didn't I tell you things were going to get a lot worse?' he says, pulling me off the roundabout. 'We got to go, Lola. We should've been home ages ago.'

Musket races across the park towards me, whimpering. I bend down and wrap my arms around his silky black neck. He licks my face.

'It's okay, boy,' I say. 'We'll be all right.'

'Come on,' Patrick says.

We sprint out of the park towards the high street, searching the grey sky as we go.

'Maybe they're just testing the sirens out. We've never had a daylight raid before,' I shout.

'Doubt it,' Patrick shouts back. 'This is for real, I reckon.'

'We need to hide. We shouldn't be out in the open.'

He shakes his head. 'Can't risk my mum coming out to look for me. We should have enough time to get home.'

Every shop we pass is empty or boarded-up, except for the newsagents. That's been renamed The Depot and it's where we pick up our weekly food boxes; although I use the word 'food' loosely – it's usually just a bag of porridge, tinned meat or fruit, disgusting bread and packets of dried soup.

We arrive, panting, at Patrick's road. A burned-out taxi, still smouldering, is parked halfway across it.

'Billy and his mates,' I say.

'Yeah, crazy.'

Billy is only about twelve, but he scares me. He's turned kind of feral – along with a few other kids who've lost their parents: looting, fighting, setting light to stuff. As if we haven't got enough to fear.

I hold out my hand to Patrick and our fingers link. His glasses are slightly askew, and he looks thin and scared.

'Keep safe,' I say.

'And you,' he nods.

There's nothing else to say.

He turns and sprints towards his house, the only one on the road still occupied – and still standing. It's like a lonely statue, exposed and surrounded by the remains of a once-busy street. Cars sit abandoned and broken, and the road is covered in the rubble and belongings of the homes that once flanked it. It's a horrible image. I turn away. Musket licks my hand, and I start jogging again. I have to get home.

After only a few steps, a thick plume of dust from a pile of debris caught up in the gathering wind swirls over me. It scratches my eyes and carries the familiar sickly stench of them – the ships. It never disappears, just hangs in the air and sticks to your every breath. I lift my hand and cover my nose – the taste of it in my mouth. I splutter and spit it out, gagging so hard I almost throw up on the pavement. Now I can taste bile in the back of my throat, burning, making me retch again.

Not looking where I'm going, I slam into someone else running in the opposite direction. We both stumble backwards. It's a boy about my age, his dark hair flapping in the wind. Not someone I know. And that's strange because I know everyone in the town. Everyone that's left.

'S-sorry,' I shout over the sirens. 'I'm so sorry.'

I look up at him when he doesn't answer. I'm not sure whether my jaw physically drops, or if it just feels like it. Because the eyes that are staring back at me are unbelievable. They don't seem real. They are the colour of fire – the deepest orange with the blackest centre. Musket is snarling beside me.

I hear him gasp as he stares at my shocked expression.

His own mouth opens as if to speak, but he doesn't. Instead he turns and runs into the dust and the wind, his head low.

Eyes like fire? That's stupid. I'm losing my mind, like everyone else. But who *was* he?

Through the wind I hear my name screamed from somewhere ahead of me.

'Mum!' I yell, running towards the sound of her voice. Mum never goes out, let alone when a raid is on.

She looms out of the dust in front of me, her face manic and her eyes wide. Her hands clamp my arms to my body.

'Where the hell have you been? School finished hours ago,' she says.

'I-I . . .'

'Have you seen your father?'

'No, I was at the playground. Why, where is he?'

'He's out looking for you!' Her hands tighten painfully around my arms. 'The sirens went off and he panicked because you weren't here. You should have been home, Lola.'

I pull away from her and run back the way I came. Mum yells after me, her voice merging into the high-pitched whine of the sirens. Musket is running ahead, barking. He knows exactly where we're going. The school. It isn't far, but as we get nearer, the ground begins to shake.

They're here.

'No!'

Vibrating the ground is what they do, driving people from their homes so they can be taken. I struggle to stay on my feet, legs like jelly, every nerve in my body pulsing on red alert. I hang on to a nearby wall, trying to breathe, to focus on the deserted road ahead. The school rises up at the end of it like a giant fortress.

'Dad!' I call.

And then I see a familiar figure by the school gates. It's him. I'd recognise his bulky frame anywhere. He's waving his arms and half-running, half-limping, towards me. He's smiling with relief. I take a step forwards, then stop.

A dark shape emerges from behind the school. It has a black outer shell – curved and hard – and in the centre, a large yellow light glowing like the eye of a predator. It looks like a flying beetle – one the size of a jumbo jet. A funnel underneath sweeps the ground, ready to suck up whatever is in its path. I call them Leeches – because they're sucking the lifeblood from the Earth. Others call them Sweepers. Ships so silent you have no choice but to listen to the final screams of their victims. And now there's one gliding over the school roof towards my dad.

Dad glances over his shoulder. He picks up speed but stumbles. The Leech is almost on top of him, the funnel reaching out . . .

'Lola . . . Sapphire . . . find it, and . . .' Dad cries out, but his hands fly to his ears and he stops, suddenly rigid. The Leech is doing something with sound. Sending out some kind of venomous pulse that is paralysing Dad before . . .

I've seen it happen – I know what it means.

'No!'

I start towards him, but two arms grab me around the waist.

'Mum, what are you doing?' I cry, struggling to break free of her grip. 'He's going to get taken!'

She's crying, sobbing words into my hair. 'You can't help him, Lola. It's too late.'

'Dad!' I scream, fighting desperately, my throat ripped raw by the force of my terror.

And then, as I watch, the funnel sweeps over him, sucking him up and into the black belly of the ship.

Chapter Two

Musket is going crazy. Mum is crying and shaking. I just feel numb. My dad, my amazing dad, is gone – and it's my fault. What have I done?

But there's no time to think about it because the ship is still moving down the street towards us. A bolt of white light shoots from the Leech's nose, skimming over our heads and into the distance. The ground trembles as an explosion erupts from the other end of the street, sending a massive wall of smoke and grit hurtling towards us. It snaps me back to my senses. We turn away, cowering, shielding ourselves from the onslaught of debris.

Musket runs around us, barking, urging us to go.

I know we need to move, but my legs won't work and my head is pounding. I know we're goners if the ship's scanners detect us. If it gets within ten metres of us, like it did with Dad, we'll be paralysed, helpless. We have to move, but the pain in my head is killing me. I can't think straight, crazy thoughts and images. My mind is being tortured by something – by them. Mum is gripping her head. She cries out, falling to her knees.

'Mum, get up,' I shout. Musket is snarling at the approaching Leech. Then I hear a voice behind me.

'Quickly!'

I look round and gasp. It's the strange boy again. His fiery eyes are bright in the dirty air. I didn't imagine him. He's *real*. But what's he doing here?

He wraps one arm around Mum's waist and the other around my shoulders, pulling us to our feet. There's a crash to my right – another house has collapsed. My ankle twists on a piece of rubble and I stumble. The pain in my head is unbearable now, like hundreds of people screaming to get out.

'Stop it!' My hands clamp over my ears, trying to silence the sound, which feels as if it's clawing down the inside of my face.

'Try to block it out,' he says. 'They're planting fear. It's what they do. Think of anything, another memory, a time when you felt happy, safe . . .' His words are sharp, clipped and direct, in perfect English – too perfect in this chaos.

I try to do as he says. I think of my playground, of Patrick. The day Mum gave me Musket, wrapped up in her coat like a furry lining. Riding my bike really fast.

The pain recedes, and suddenly the boy is lifting me off the ground and running towards my house. Mum is

already there, struggling to open the door, Musket barking at her feet.

'It'll be over soon,' the boy says as he lowers me to the
ground. Those orange eyes . . . They're freaking me out
big time.

'Who are you?'

'Come on,' Mum yells, waving frantically. 'Both of
you.'

He shakes his head. 'I can't. But you must go inside,
now.'

I haven't time to say thank you before he turns and
runs across the street – disappearing like a ghost into the
murky gloom.

We don't utter a word in the shelter – a tiny room beneath
the kitchen that Dad built when the raids first started. It
even has a tunnel to the garden, just in case the house
collapses. It's freezing and damp.

I listen to the explosions outside and the constant
rumbling as the ground vibrates around us. I try not to
imagine what's happening. Try not to think about who's
being taken.

Huddled on a lumpy cushion, a blanket draped around
my shoulders, I can't stop shivering, or the tears from
streaming down my cheeks. Dad is gone. I can't believe it.
I don't want to believe it. I keep thinking about what he
called out after my name – sapphire – but I don't understand what he meant.

In the dim light, Mum looks like a corpse. Her eyes are
sunken and ringed with darkness. Everyone has that gaunt

look now; I guess I do too. Lack of food equals lack of flesh. I just hope my eyes don't become empty like hers.

'You should have let me go after him,' I say.

She looks at me, her cheeks shiny and wet. 'You couldn't have saved him, Lola. It would have been suicide to try.'

I lean my head back against the wall and try to control my breathing. I didn't know I was claustrophobic until after the shelter had been built. During a midnight raid we'd all crammed in for the first time. I didn't fear the Leeches that night, just my own stupid body conking out on me. Now it's just me and Mum, and the fear is gripping me worse than ever. I crave Dad's soothing voice. The words he'd always say to me when I was feeling down. The words he'd say to me right now if he were here – 'Chin up, Lola. It's not that bad.' I close my eyes at the thought of never hearing them again.

'Use this if you feel panicky, sweetheart,' Mum says, handing me a paper bag. 'The raid will be over soon.'

I nod and lift the bag to my mouth, breathing into it deeply and slowly. Two large torches hang from the ceiling, swinging as the ground vibrates. They give off some light but fail to stop it feeling as if the walls are closing in, and their constant swaying makes me feel seasick.

One wall of the shelter is stacked high with tins of food and bottled water, just in case we have to stay down here for a long time – a thought that terrifies me. I've never even heard of some of the tins' contents, let alone eaten them. Mum gets a few things cheap from Bill Turner at number three. I dread to think where he gets them. But no one asks questions anymore – best not to.

Food is getting scarce and everyone has their special ration tokens for The Depot, but they don't stretch very far. I try to remember life before the raids, what it was like to eat fresh fruit. The crunch of an apple, or the juice of a peach. And chocolate . . . I haven't had chocolate for years. No one dares to think about the day when there will be nothing left to eat. But that day is getting closer.

Musket lays his head across my lap, glancing up at me every now and again as if to check I'm okay – which, of course, I'm not. My head is still throbbing, and I can't stop thinking about Dad.

And the stranger. I've often wondered if the terrible headaches we get during raids and the nightmares that follow are some kind of mind control. What was it he said? *They're planting fear – it's what they do.* How come he knew that? Is he one of the monsters? We don't know what they look like and can only imagine what it's like inside their ships. No one has ever come back to tell us.

Mum hasn't mentioned the boy. I think she's glad he didn't accept her offer to join us. I know she's scared of who, or what, he might be. But he did help us.

The hours pass and still the ground shakes. One of the torch beams is flickering, and we're down to the last of our batteries. Please, please don't go out. Mum is silent. I pull the blanket tighter around myself as it gets colder and darker. The torchlight finally loses its battle and dies.

Is that what will happen to us?

I remember when we all used to fight back. Now we do nothing except wait. Information isn't easy to get. The TV and internet went first, and no one really believes the radio reports we still receive – they sound so false and rehearsed. Is the rest of the world still fighting? Or just surviving day to day, like us? The Prime Minister used to deliver grand speeches about how we would never give up, how every country was going to unite against our attackers. But those speeches stopped a long time ago, and now we're told nothing of any importance. Instead we're fed boring reports about fallen historical buildings or the latest celebrity who's been taken, as if their lives are more important than ours. But I won't give up. Dad always had hope. And so do I.

I cry myself to sleep, listening as the raid goes on and on.

Something on the ceiling is moving, sliding towards me. The smell is rancid, like rotting meat. A layer of grey slime, like a slow-moving river, puddles on the floor, covering my school shoes. I stumble back, gagging and shivering. It is painfully cold. Clouds of white breath swirl from my mouth as I listen for the rasping, squelching sound. It's here. It's always here.

My heart hurts as it pounds against my ribs. I don't want to look up, because I know what's there, what's coming – but it's the only way to end this nightmare. Every muscle tightens as I sense it looming above me, like a giant slug. I force my head to look up and for a split second I see it: a diamond-shaped mouth full of razor-sharp teeth stretching out towards me . . .

And then I'm screaming, gasping for breath, my hands clawing at the blanket.

'It's all right, Lola, I'm here. It's only the nightmare. It's over.'

'I don't want to die like that, I don't want to,' I cry.

'Ssh, it's not real. You're awake now.'

Mum grips me by the shoulders, and my shaking and breathing gradually calm down. But the nightmare always feels real, however many times I have it. I'm soaked in sweat, and tears fall freely down my face.

'Where are they, Mum?' I cry. 'Aunty Helen, Mal, Lucy, Faye, Ricky, Aleeza, Mrs Dawson, Callum and now Dad . . . I can't even remember them all anymore, there're too many.'

'They've gone, sweetheart.' She sweeps her hand over my wet cheek. 'You don't need to remember them all, it doesn't matter.'

'It *does* matter. We can't just forget them!'

She looks at the floor. She hates me being like this, I know she does.

'The raid's over. We'd better go up.' She gets to her feet and opens the trapdoor.

'Mum?'

'Yes, sweetheart?'

'That boy said the creatures mess with our heads. I think they might plant the nightmares to scare us, to keep us from fighting back. It would make sense, wouldn't it?'

She stares at me, fear clouding her tired eyes. 'He's one of them. They look human. I knew it. My God, there could be hundreds of them walking around and we'd never know.'

I don't reply, but I'm thinking the same thing. Then, holding hands, we venture outside.

Chapter Three

It's morning. I can't believe the raid went on all night, and that I stayed down in the shelter all that time. The wind has dropped and the sun is shining, although the world still looks grey somehow – devastation doesn't seem to come in any other colour.

It's a bad one this time, maybe the worst ever, and the closest to our home. I stand at my front door, staring at the five houses on the other side of the street, which are now piles of smoking rubble. My stomach twists at the thought of what's happened. The nine people who once lived in them – all gone. Either buried alive or taken.

I walk over to Musket who is sniffing at something – a red shoe lying in the gutter. I bend down and pick it up. It's dirty and the buckle is broken. But the worst thing is I know who it belongs to. I remember her showing them to me when they were shiny and new. Claudia Rose. She's only five. I spit on my finger and try to wipe the dirt off the toe, but it's engrained and scuffed. It won't shine anymore. I throw it down.

I hate this. Why don't we fight back?

'Lola!' I turn and see Patrick running towards me. 'Are you okay? I just heard about your dad. I spoke to someone who saw the whole thing. I'm so, so sorry.' Tears fill his eyes.

'I still can't accept he's gone.'

'I know,' Patrick says, rubbing my shoulder. It feels a bit awkward; me and Patrick don't normally do touchy-feely, although he does try sometimes. 'He was the best, you know. A top guy.'

'He still is,' I snap. 'He isn't dead.'

It makes me so mad how everyone assumes you die when you're taken. I don't, and nor did Dad.

'Lola, I—'

'Don't say anything, Patrick. I don't want pity.'

'I'm sorry,' he says.

I stare at the rubble. Why do we still know so little? Some of the Leeches were shot down during the first raids, giving us some information about them. Dad works for the government as a scientist. He told me they'd got a substance from the Leeches' fuel that they were using to make a weapon – a weapon that would allow us to finally fight back and win. But that was ages ago, and still we wait. I guess it didn't work.

There were never any creatures on board the Leeches

that were shot down – or maybe there were? The humans they found trapped inside were dead from the impact, but some could have been like the boy with the fire in his eyes. Maybe they do something to us and then use us as pilots. I shake my head; that's a crazy idea, but it's torture not knowing the truth, or who to fear.

I feel a tug at the back of my school blazer. I turn to see Aimee, the little girl who lives next door to me. She's seven with bright-red hair.

'Lola, please can I take Musket for a walk?' she asks. 'I'll look after him – promise. He can play ball with me and Mr Topsy.' She points to the small bundle of fluff sitting beside her feet.

My hand goes automatically to Musket's lead. 'Um, not really, Aimee. Musket stays with me.'

'But I'll bring him straight back to your house after. Please, Lola.'

I frown. 'And your mum lets you go out on your own?' I can't believe her mum allows her so much freedom when mine allows me none, and I'm fourteen.

'Yeah, she always lets me.'

'Right, well . . .' I look down at Musket. His tail is wagging at full speed. I think he knows what we're talking about. And he does deserve a walk after being cooped up all night. I hand Aimee the lead. 'Okay then, but keep him on his lead, and bring him home in ten minutes.'

'Thanks, Lola. You're the best.'

I watch as she skips off through the rubble, Musket on one side and Mr Topsy on the other. She seems so carefree – but then Aimee doesn't really remember a life before the raids. For her, this is normal.

Mum walks over to me, her arms gripped across her chest as if trying to keep out reality. 'I'm making breakfast – you coming in?' Her tone is bland, like she's immune to the death in the air.

'Not hungry,' I reply.

'You need to eat, Lola,' she frowns. 'Hello, Patrick.'

'Mrs Hubbard,' he nods. 'I'm sorry about—'

'There's no need. We've all lost people we love,' she says. I hear her take a deep breath. 'Lola, the roof of your father's workshop has collapsed . . .'

'What?' I gasp.

Her expression is tense; she knows how much Dad's workshop means to me. It's just a shed in the garden, but it's where he's been working ever since the Government's science labs closed down, and he was developing something important there – he just didn't tell us what it was. If I asked him he would change the subject. When I knocked on the door I'd hear him shuffling papers and clearing things away. He would work late into the night, not eating or sleeping unless we forced him to.

But his workshop was always the place, the only place, where me and him really talked. Secret stuff, personal stuff, silly stuff.

I bolt into our back garden. The roof of the shed is crushed, like a giant has sat down on it. My heart dips at the sight of the small wooden structure leaning to one side, as if in pain. Why do they have to destroy everything?

'Lola.' Patrick is behind me. 'Do you want me to come in with you?'

'No, I'll be fine.' I knew I'd want to come here today; but I didn't think I'd feel this bad. 'I'll be out in a minute. I just . . . need to check everything is okay.'

I reach out and touch the handle. My hand lingers on the cold rusty metal and my heart beats faster. I slowly push open the door as far as the collapsed roof will allow, and squeeze inside. I have to stoop. Luckily not too much has been destroyed. A shelf has come loose from the wall and paperwork lies in messy heaps on the floor.

Light floods the room from a skylight at the far end, its glass blown in, the fragments glittering on the desk and the ground around it. The place looks different now, and there is a cold emptiness which never existed before. It's horrible to be here without Dad.

At one end of the shed is a table covered in scientific equipment. Numerous jars of chemicals are lined up on shelves above. Some are smashed, their brightly coloured contents spilled on to the floor. Rows of books line another wall, so tightly packed together they haven't budged. His desk is tidy, as it always is.

Amongst the shards of broken glass from the window are piles of papers. They sit neatly together, each document separated with coloured paper clips. I smile to myself. I always teased him about his obsession with paper clips.

Dad's reading glasses are lying on top of his leather notebook, as if he's just nipped out for something. He must have been here when the sirens went off. When I wasn't home. I pick up the black, half-moon glasses and fold the arms in, trying to ignore the pain in my chest and the pressure building behind my eyes. As I lay them back down, I notice a letter lying beneath the spine of the book.

It's the official government logo that first catches my eye. I know I shouldn't read it, but it's been ages since I've seen anything official looking. And a letter from the government is proof they still exist, that we're still being looked after. I pick it up. A small breath catches at the back of my throat as I scan the print.

'No longer require your services . . . please discontinue all further developments of Project Sapphire with immediate effect . . . Do not attempt to make any further contact with us . . .'

I slowly sit down in dad's leather chair, his coat still slung across the back of it. I lay the letter back on the desk. It is dated six months ago. Why would he say he was still working for the government if it wasn't true? I knew the government buildings had closed, but Dad said he was continuing their work from home. Why did he lie? And why was he fired? I knew he'd fallen out with a few people, but . . .

'Project Sapphire,' I whisper. That's what he called out to me, just before he was taken. He shouted that for a reason. He wanted me to find it. But what is it? I stand up and search the top of his desk, pulling papers from their orderly rows. My heart is quickening. I grab his coat and squeeze the left pocket – nothing. I plough my hand into the right pocket and my fingers close around something. I take it out. It's a small, slim blue pot. On the lid is a symbol of a blue sapphire.

'Patrick,' I shout. Suddenly I'm shaking.

The door grinds opens and Patrick stumbles in, frowning. 'What's wrong, mate?'

I unscrew the top of the pot and tip the contents on to my palm. Two small white capsules fall out, each one with a red tip. I stare at them. They seem so ordinary, like something you'd take for a headache, but I'm guessing they're not painkillers.

'Dad wanted me to find these. What are they?'

'Pills,' Patrick says. 'Was he ill?'

'No, I don't think so. It was something he was working on.' I place the pills on the desk and show Patrick the letter. Then I see something lying between the dishevelled papers – a pale blue folder. I pull it out, the same sapphire symbol is emblazoned on the front. I look at Patrick, but he's already noticed it.

He takes it from me and sits in Dad's chair. He flicks through the pages and then stops. His forehead creases. I try and read over his shoulder, but I don't understand any of what I'm seeing. Symbols and numbers in Dad's untidy scrawl. I've never been any good at science.

After what seems like an age, Patrick closes the file and places it back down on the desk. He looks pale and solemn. 'Those pills are the weapon your dad was developing for the government, only they don't want it anymore,' he says.

'But they're just pills . . .'

'No, Lola, they're bombs,' he says, his head shaking in disbelief. 'They're supposed to act as a deterrent. If you're going to get taken then you swallow the pill. According to your dad's notes, when the substance inside mixes with any human fluid, it explodes. He's calculated that one pill is the exact amount needed for it to work. It's gruesome. But I guess if you're going to die anyway you may as well destroy the thing that's killing you. I think the idea is that if the attackers know we all have them, then maybe they'll think twice about taking us.'

'But we don't know that our attackers kill the people they take.'

Patrick shrugs. 'Then we should leave well alone. This isn't our business.'

But my dad's business is my business. 'Does it say anything else?'

'No, just loads of formulations on how to make more pills, and notes on how this could save the human race from extinction.'

I feel sick as I look at the pills. The thought of what they could do sends a shiver through me and I tip them back into the pot. It's hard to believe they're as powerful as Patrick says. But if Dad believed in them, then why didn't the government?

My mind is whizzing. I need to think. Why did Dad shout those words to me? Perhaps he needed the pills. They were in his coat, and he didn't take his coat because he left in a hurry to look for me. Maybe he has a plan. Maybe the pills don't need to be swallowed. What if there's another way to use them?

'We should go, Lola,' Patrick says. 'Forget we saw any of this stuff.'

'But someone needs to find Dad's work. They need to

know about it,' I say.

'From what I can gather from the notes, your dad was working alone. There could be a good reason the government aren't interested. Leave it.'

But I'm not listening. I'm trying to keep calm, panic only seconds away. I look across at the folder. Everything to do with Project Sapphire is in there. But if the government don't want it, then who do I trust? I shove the folder under the pile of papers again. This is the safest place for it to stay for now. Maybe Mum will know what to do, who to take it to. One of Dad's friends, maybe?

I stuff the blue pot into my blazer pocket.

'What are you doing with that?' Patrick says. 'Leave it here.'

'I think I should give it to Mum to look after. It'll be safer in the house.'

He looks at me over the top of his ever-crooked glasses. 'I'd rather you just got rid of it. Those things freak me out.'

'I will,' I say, trying to sound in control even though my insides are twisting into knots.

I have to help Dad. He wants me to take the pot to him, I know he does. Why else would he tell me to find it? I'm his back-up plan. I'll tell Mum about the folder – she'll know who to trust. Then we fight back. We take the fight to the Leeches.

Now all I have to do is wait for the next raid.

Chapter Four

We walk back round to the front of the house. I can't tell Patrick what I'm planning to do. He'd try and stop me, and I don't want to fall out with him – especially if this ends up being our last few days together. Patrick was close to my dad, they'd sit for hours discussing scientific stuff, and Patrick (being the cleverest person in the world), understood it all. But he wouldn't understand this.

The crowd around the ruined houses has doubled, twenty at least. PC Jackleson is trying to keep people back, as well as having a very animated argument with Mr Willis, who used to own the corner shop – when there was a corner shop. From what I can gather people want to dig for survivors, but PC Jackleson is telling them it's too dangerous. What a joke. I'm surprised they still listen to him. He's the only policeman we have left. Mum says it's good of him to continue and to want to retain some kind of order in the town. And people *are* listening to him, because the crowd is deathly quiet – apart from Mr Willis, that is. Occasionally they edge their scrawny frames closer to the rubble, only to protest in whispers when they're ushered back by PC Jackleson's flailing arms. They're nothing more than shadows – spiritless shadows.

I jump as a car horn rents the air. An army truck rumbles towards us and stops on the other side of the rubble mounds. Two soldiers with guns slung over their shoulders jump out.

'Everyone is to back away and leave,' one of the soldiers demands, stony-faced.

The crowd shrinks away, cowering. Their already stooped shoulders slump a little lower. I want to grab them all and shake them. Why are they scared of these soldiers? They're on our side – aren't they?

'Let's get out of here,' Patrick says. He tries to pull me away.

'Wait,' I say, twisting out of his grasp. Suddenly I'm clambering over bricks and pieces of broken furniture, towards one of the soldiers. I need some answers and maybe he can give them to me.

He raises his gun, his expression wary. 'I said back away.'

I stop. The other one is staring at me too. They're both wearing long chains around their necks with a red sphere pendant attached, covered in gold markings. I've noticed them before, but I don't know what they are. Even Dad didn't know. Maybe it's a new kind of ranking system.

'I want to know if there's still someone in charge,' I shout, my heart pounding in my ears.

Patrick is by my side again. 'Lola, what are you playing at?'

'Ssh.' I take another wobbly step forwards, but Patrick places a firm hand on my shoulder.

'You know there's a government,' the soldier answers.

'Then why don't they make you attack the ships anymore? Why come here with your guns and threaten us, but do nothing to stop the monsters that did this?'

I hear a faint ripple of agreement from the small crowd and to my shock a lone clap from Mr Willis.

The soldier stiffens and steps closer. I can see down the barrel of the gun and I just know that this man will use it if I utter another word.

'Enough,' he spits.

I let Patrick win, allowing him to pull me back as the crowd groan their disapproval at the soldier.

I look back over my shoulder as we walk away. 'Why are they even here anyway? Worried we're going to do some looting? Or maybe they don't want us to find any survivors. It's stupid. Never around when we do need them. Probably all hiding in their bunker with the Prime Minister and letting the rest of us get picked off one by one. Did you hear the crowd? They were on my side. It was like I woke them up or something. Told you not everyone wants to give up.'

'Lola, stop it. What's got into you? They're here to stop

28

people getting hurt. It's their job to dig through the rubble, not ours. They're trained for that sort of thing.' Patrick shakes his head. 'And what was all that about the government? You're not still thinking about that letter?'

'No, of course not,' I mumble. I feel the lump of the pot in my blazer pocket.

'Good, cos you're scaring me. Anyway, where are we going? I can't believe your mum actually expects you to go to school after . . . after yesterday.'

'She doesn't. But if I don't go to school she'll make me stay at home all day and I can't bear it. She won't let me go anywhere else, you know that.'

There's no logic in Mum's thinking, she just seems to think school is safe because it's never been attacked . . . yet. I don't know whether to tell Patrick about the stranger from yesterday. I decide to do it later, when he's in the right mood. He doesn't like talking about our attackers.

We're halfway along the high street and heading in the direction of our playground, even though neither of us has said that's where we're going. I like it when me and Patrick are so in tune we don't have to speak. I'll miss him so much when I leave, but I have no choice. I have to help Dad and the only way to do that is to get taken. Although the thought of being sucked up that funnel is terrifying. And will I even be able to find Dad? I don't know, but I have to try, even if that means dying in the attempt. And then there's Musket. What will I do without Musket? I hate the thought of leaving him behind. Mum doesn't even like him — what if she kicks him out?

A lone scream pierces the air. We stop. Silence falls. No birds, no wind, nothing. It's like the Earth is holding its breath.

'This isn't good,' Patrick whispers.

'It can't be another raid,' I say.

We both stand rigidly in the centre of the road. Then, to our left, over the rooftops of the boarded-up shops, we see a Leech.

Patrick gasps and we both instinctively duck, even though it's not heading our way.

'Since when do we not get sirens anymore?' I say.

'And since when do we get two raids straight after one another?'

'Maybe they destroyed the siren station yesterday,' I say, trying not to panic.

I watch as the Leech heads away, turning towards the edge of town.

'Musket! Where did Aimee take Musket?' I shout, grabbing Patrick's arm.

'Hey, watch it. I don't know — maybe she took him back to yours already.'

I start running. If this is a raid, then what do I do? I was hoping for more time to plan things properly, think it through. I'll find Musket first, and then decide.

'Lola, slow down,' Patrick cries from behind.

I'm back at my road. The crowd has gone but the soldiers are still there, seemingly unfazed. Maybe they didn't see the Leech.

I go round to the back of the house, passing Dad's workshop. 'Please be here,' I whisper as I open the kitchen door. I can't even think about leaving unless I know Musket is safe. 'Why did I let him go with Aimee?'

'He'll be fine,' Patrick says, following me in.

'Musket,' I cry, almost tripping over his basket by the door. 'Where are you?'

The kitchen is empty, as is the lounge. My heavy footsteps don't go unnoticed. As I run back into the hall, Mum comes down the stairs.

'Lola, Patrick — what are you doing back?' she says, looking surprised. 'Why aren't you at school?'

'Has Aimee brought Musket home?'

'Aimee? Musket? What are you talking about? No she hasn't.'

I feel sick. Don't panic, I think. They're probably safe somewhere — hiding out.

'I have to find him.'

'Find who? Musket?' She stares at me, her face so taut it looks as if her skin might split. I know she doesn't understand.

'I'll check Aimee's house,' Patrick says, dashing out of the door.

'Mum, there are Leeches out there, I need to find him.'

'What are you talking about? There isn't a raid on — there aren't any sirens. And it's only been a few hours since the last one,' she says.

'I know what I saw. It was a Leech and it flew over the town.'

Mum's face drains of the little colour it has. 'Then we should get into the shelter.'

'I can't, I have to find Musket.'

31

'No, Lola, that dog isn't worth it.'

'Well, according to you, Dad wasn't worth it either,' I snap. 'I'm going to look for Musket, and then for Dad too.'

Mum runs to the front door and blocks my escape. She takes my hand, her face inches from mine. 'I'm not losing you too, I couldn't bear it.'

'You're not stopping me, Mum. I could have saved Dad yesterday, only you wouldn't let me. I'm not listening to you this time, and I'm not losing Musket either.' I try to twist out of her grip. 'If Dad's dead then you killed him.'

As soon as the words tumble from my mouth, I know I've gone too far. Mum's hand falls to her side, releasing me. I can't say anything now to put this right. I push past her and run from the house.

Patrick comes out of Aimee's house, shaking his head.

'The common,' I shout, ignoring the soldiers as we run. 'If she took him to play ball, then that's where they'll be.'

I stop at the entrance to the common by the tall iron gates and the lichen-covered statue of some old politician. My palms are all clammy, yesterday's attack is still raw, and I'm trying to forget what I've said to Mum. I can hear desperate cries. The ground is trembling again, like the whole planet is being shaken by a giant hand.

I can't think straight, but I know I'm running out of time.

'Patrick . . .'

He turns to me. 'What?'

'If anything happens to me I want you to take care of Musket.' I link our fingers together. 'Promise me.'

He stares at me, his face full of confusion. 'I promise. But nothing is going to happen to you. Why say that?'

'And tell Mum about the folder we found. She knows some of Dad's friends, maybe who to go to.'

'Lola . . . what are you going on about?'

To my relief, something grabs his attention. I follow his gaze upwards. In the distance, heading our way, is a Leech. No sound, just a huge black mound of metal, like a giant bug with its piercing yellow eye.

'I need to find Musket. Where is he?'

'No, we need to stay alive, Lola. We've got to get out of here – like now.'

'But I have to find him.'

And yet . . . I want to go. I want to find Dad. Only now I'm not so sure I can go through with it – it's too soon. I should wait for the next raid, that's what I should do. Be better prepared. But better prepared for what? I have no idea what I'm facing. I have to get the pills to Dad, that's my plan. Will waiting for the next raid make any difference? Maybe I should be taking supplies with me – food, a knife . . .

The Leech is getting closer, sweeping over the small river and woodland that surround the common. The pain in my head is back and by the look on Patrick's face, he's suffering too. We're too close to the Leech. I hear a high-pitched yap coming from the trees and I see Mr Topsy sprint from the woods – a little brown ball of fluff zooming across the grass like an overgrown rat. I hear Aimee screaming his name, and then I freeze. Musket is bolting after him, straight into the path of the Leech.

'Musket!' I screech.

He stops to look at me but gets distracted again when Aimee runs out.

I don't think. I take a step forwards, then another and now I'm running. Musket doesn't know what to do. But I do. This time no one is holding me back, begging me to stay away from it. The Leech is sweeping low across the common.

'Aimee, go back!'

She stops, but doesn't look at me. A man runs out from the trees to help her. The Leech is so close I can smell it – that sweet, sickly stench. Below its belly, the funnel is just a few metres from the ground. It sweeps over Mr Topsy. He disappears, sucked from the surface like a piece of dust from a carpet.

'Musket, come here,' I yell.

He tries to run but he can't move. I'm too late, just like with Dad. The funnel creeps towards him, like a gaping metal mouth looking for its lunch.

'No!' I scream. 'Please, no.'

My stomach curls and I collapse to the ground in agony.

The funnel is over him and then, he's snapped from the surface before I can make another sound. Musket is gone.

Someone yanks me to my feet. 'Come on,' Patrick shouts.

The Leech starts heading in my direction. Can I do this? Yes, they have Musket now as well as Dad – I have to. My heart is racing so fast I feel dizzy. This is it. My fate isn't here, just surviving. It's up there, helping to end this.

'Lola . . .' Patrick is dragging me away.

'Go home, Patrick, get out of here.' I push him with as much force as I can muster.

'I'm not leaving you.'

'This is my choice, now go . . . please.'

The Leech turns towards the trees. 'No, it's not leaving me here.'

I run for it, my legs buckling with every determined stride, but I keep going. And then, to my weird relief, the giant machine slowly changes direction back to me.

I stop and look up at the massive funnel edging ever nearer. I spin round and see Patrick still shouting at me, a horrified expression on his face.

'Run, you idiot!' I scream.

Then in the distance, by the trees, I see him again – the stranger, the boy with the fire in his eyes. He's not moving, just staring at me. His hands grip the top of his head as if he's trying to crush it. I blink hard, my head feeling woozy as the dark shadow looms over me. I spin back round and fall to the ground, my fingers clawing at the grass.

I'm so scared. I clench my whole body and grit my teeth so hard my jaw hurts. This is it.

And then it happens. Pain, terrible pain, tears its way through my skull. But all I can think about is Dad. Did he survive this, or am I about to die too? I can't move. Every limb is stiff and numb. My breath jams in my throat and blinding blackness fills my vision.

Then I'm sucked away from the Earth.

All my breath is whipped from my body as I soar

upwards into the dark. Stretched and twisted like a piece of rubber. I can't see anything as I hurtle, head first, like a rollercoaster in a tunnel. I still can't feel my body, but my mind is frantic. Mum, Dad, Patrick, Musket, they're all flitting in and out of my head. Random images that make no sense at all.

And in the middle of them all, the realisation that I've got what I wanted. I've been taken.

Chapter Five

A soothing whoosh of warm air engulfs me and I'm flung on to something soft. Before I have time to think, the ground tips and I'm rolling down on to a rough, hot surface.

It presses painfully into my cheek. I can't get my bearings, I don't know which way is up, or which way is down. But I'm no longer paralysed. I blink, trying to focus on something – anything.

Although dimly lit, I slowly begin to realise I'm in a cavernous black space – it must be the belly of the ship. Its sickly smell is unmistakable. I touch my chest. It feels as if my lungs want to tear with every intake of air. I retch, unable to stop my stomach from cramping.

When I look up, I realise something else. I'm not

alone. There are people all around me. The people who have just been taken. We stare at each other.

A woman scurries over and drapes a long, sweaty arm across my shoulders. 'Come on, luv, you'll be okay in a minute. Sit with me.'

I stare up at her and try to swallow the hard, dry lump in my throat. Her eyes look manic. I've never seen so much fear in a person before.

Every inch of my body is in pain. And it's hot in here – really hot. My hair is already dripping with sweat and sticking to the nape of my neck. My left hand is covered in mud and grass. I sniff it, breathing in the faint smell of Earth for maybe the last time.

The woman is chewing her thumbnail. 'Oh dear, I'm so worried. I think I might have left my oven on. Do you think it'll be all right?'

I nod, but a man sitting further along then calls to her. 'Julia, leave the girl alone.' She smiles nervously at me, as if she wants to stay longer, but turns and scuttles back to the man.

And then, to my horror, a familiar voice cries out from behind me.

'Lola . . . Lola, where are you?'

'Patrick!' His body rolls into mine. 'I-I told you to run.'

'I went to help Aimee – didn't quite make it,' he groans, twisting the ball of his palm into his forehead. His glasses are bent to one side, but still intact.

'Did she . . . Is she all right?'

He shakes his head. 'Don't know. Can't believe you just did that, Lola. I know you love Musket, but going after him was just mental.'

'I had no choice. I needed to . . . I need to know what's going on,' I say.

'Yeah, well, you'll know soon enough,' he coughs. 'We all will.'

'You sure you're okay?' I ask him.

'I guess, but breathing is . . .'

'I know. I think our lungs were crushed. Take little breaths – it helps.'

We settle down as best we can and wait as more people roll down the slope. I can see the slope more clearly as my eyes adjust to the gloom. It's wide and reaches half-way up the wall. At the top is an inlet and I can hear the constant tipping motion as it throws people down the slope to the floor. My heart sinks into my shoes when I see little Aimee amongst the latest batch.

'No, this isn't happening. Why didn't you all get away?' I cry. 'It should just be me.'

'The common wasn't the best . . . the best place to try and hide,' Patrick says. 'I can't believe this. We've been taken, Lola. It's game over.'

As I shuffle back towards the wall, Aimee crawls over, sobbing and presses her body to mine. Her laboured breaths match my own.

'What happened? I'm really scared, Lola.'

'Don't worry.' I stroke her fringe back from her forehead. A bloody graze covers half her cheek. 'Does that hurt?'

'A bit,' she mumbles. 'I fell over trying to run. My tummy hurts more, though.'

'Mine too.'

'I-I'm sorry about Musket. I was going to take him home, but—'

'Hey, don't worry. We'll find him, and Mr Topsy.' Then it occurs to me. 'They should be in here too, surely.'

I scan the cavern. 'Musket,' I yell, wincing and holding a hand to my chest as a sharp pain shoots through my lungs. My voice echoes around the walls and all eyes turn on me. Silence falls. No Musket or Mr Topsy. 'Where are they?'

Patrick joins us. 'I don't see any animals. Maybe they get sucked up into another chute.'

'Maybe.' Musket has to be okay, he just has to be.

I'm trembling and I can't stop it, no matter how hard I try. The shock of where I am has hit me, as if I've been holding it at arm's length and then suddenly let go.

Will I ever see my home again? My mum? I have a horrible feeling I won't. I had no time to say goodbye. Patrick puts his arm around me and Aimee cuddles in tighter. We're like a little family, clinging together.

'You're hugging me, Patrick,' I whisper, but I don't pull away. It feels nice – safe.

'Yeah,' he answers, and his voice is trembling too. 'Hope you don't mind.'

'No.'

They're terrified, and I wish they weren't here. But this is what I wanted, isn't it? I did this on purpose, to find Dad. There will be no more waiting for answers. No more wondering about the creatures that torment us.

'At least we're still alive,' I say, trying my hardest to

produce a positive from somewhere.

'For now,' Patrick mutters.

'Just think, maybe they're taking us to a whole new world. All our stupid fears are probably for nothing, and the truth is, we're going to a much better place – a paradise.'

'Yeah, called death.'

'Don't say that,' I whisper. 'Not in front of Aimee.'

'Will you please stop being so hopeful?' I can sense his anger.

'No,' I frown. 'Humans are gonna survive this – somehow.'

'Whatever, but in three years why haven't they ever tried to speak to us?'

I shrug. Maybe they have their reasons. At least now, and with my help, Dad can make them stop and take notice. My hand touches the pot, but as I look at Patrick, I feel sick. The folder.

'Oh no.'

'What?' Patrick asks, concern sweeping across his face.

'You were supposed to tell Mum about the folder.'

'Not much I can do about that now. You did get rid of those pills, didn't you?'

'Yeah, of course. I gave the pot to Mum before I left the house.' I look away, knowing that if Patrick sees my face he'll know I'm lying.

'But you didn't think to tell her about the folder?'

'No, I didn't have time, we kind of . . . argued.'

'Probably for the best . . . Not that you argued, but you know . . . And I told you, it's not our business anyway. We should leave well alone.'

But this is bad, more than bad — catastrophic. He has no idea how crucial it was for him not to get taken, for him to give the folder to Mum. Even if I do find Dad, whatever he does will be useless, because no one on Earth will know what to do, or how to make more pills.

My hand shoots to my sweat-covered forehead as if trying to keep it from exploding. I should have stayed and talked to Mum myself; waited for a later raid. Idiot.

'We should try to get out of here,' Patrick says, oblivious to the minor breakdown I'm having beside him.

'You really think that's possible?'

He doesn't answer, but I feel his body sag beside me, like he knows it's not.

Numbness overtakes me as I try to think of a way to solve this mess. I just have to find Dad — he'll know what to do. Why did I have to mess everything up? I lay my head back until it touches the hard, uneven wall behind me. I look up into the blackness above, trying to hold on to some kind of reality. Tears roll down my face.

I'm inside a Leech, the thing that has haunted me every day for so long. The low drone radiating from the wall behind me is kind of odd, considering that from the outside they're always so quiet. I'm not sure, but it feels as if we're travelling at speed, sometimes dipping and then climbing again, but we're not being thrown around.

I've lost track of time, but it seems as though we've been sitting in silence for hours — the heat getting more and more intense, the indent at the base of my throat now a pool of warm sweat. I undo my school tie and let it hang like a scarf.

Other people join us, rolling down from the chutes, all with the same petrified look, all sobbing. Aimee has finally cried herself to sleep, and Patrick lets out a long sigh every now and again.

I try to block out every little noise and thought – I want nothingness. But I'm not allowed to stay in my dream world for long. Aimee wakes with a start as a deafening alarm screeches out around us. Stark white light bathes us from above and I cover my eyes, the harshness way too much to bear after all the hours of darkness.

'STAND,' an electronic voice says from above.

I pull Aimee to her feet. People are crying again, the fear in the room tangible. We huddle towards the centre. It's now that I can see just how many people are here – hundreds, walking in from the ship's dark corners.

The alarm stops and the lights dim again, causing a terrified gasp to weave through the crowd like a snake. I feel claustrophobic for the first time since arriving; the crowd is squeezing me on all sides. *Breathe*, I tell myself and I grip Aimee's hand a little tighter. Three large green lights appear on the back wall. I stand on tiptoe to see more. A silver coloured door glows beneath each one.

Patrick takes my other hand and we link fingers.

'I guess this is it, mate.'

'We stick together . . . right?' I smile nervously.

'Always.'

The chilling electronic voice booms out again. 'MAKE YOUR WAY TO A DOOR AND WAIT. ONE HUMAN

AT A TIME TO ENTER THE PROCESSING UNIT. INAPPROPRIATE BEHAVIOUR WILL RESULT IN THE PREMATURE ELIMINATION OF YOUR EXISTENCE.'

'Blimey,' Patrick says. 'I think we're done for.'

More hysterical cries circulate from the crowd. Some people have collapsed and are being dragged to their feet by others.

'What did that mean?' Aimee asks.

'We're dead,' Patrick answers.

I scowl at him. 'We'll be fine, Aimee. We just need to do exactly what they say . . . for now.'

People shuffle towards the doors. We go for the nearest, the one to the right hand side of us – it's as good as any, I figure. Reluctant queues form, and everyone seems to be battling their inner feelings quietly now. All three doors slide open in unison to reveal a strange red haze swirling within. My stomach lurches.

It's clear no one wants to go first. Arguments start to break out at the front. Pushing and shoving. I pull Aimee closer, trying to protect her from the chaos, until eventually a united acceptance wins over the crowd. One person from each queue walks silently towards the openings and disappears into the redness beyond, followed by the gentle thud of the doors sliding shut behind them.

'What do you reckon they mean by processing unit?' I ask Patrick.

'Dunno, but it doesn't sound like your paradise, does it?'

'No, it doesn't. But what if they take different people to different places? Dad could still be okay.' I say, wondering whether I'm trying to convince him or myself. I'd do anything for it to be true, to find Dad alive and well somewhere, and to be able to scrap his plan to use the pills. To discover it's all been one big misunderstanding and these creatures are actually welcoming us to their world. But even I have to admit, that's looking more and more unlikely.

A man wearing a white bandana covered in black skulls stares at me. He seems to snigger at my idea of a paradise. I look away; I have to keep hoping.

One by one the queues diminish and it's finally our turn. I know Aimee will have to go in by herself, but I can't bear to see her so frightened.

'I'll meet you on the other side, poppet – I promise.'

She nods, her tear-streaked cheeks so pale. I hug her tight and then grudgingly I let her go. My hand clamps over my mouth as soon as the door shuts behind her.

'I think I'm gonna be sick again.'

Patrick holds me around the waist as I retch what little contents I have in my stomach on to the floor. 'You shouldn't have promised her, Lola. What if you don't see her on the other side?'

'T-then I'll find her, somehow,' I splutter, straightening up and wiping my sleeve across my face. Manners aren't top of my priorities right now.

'Is that after or before you've found your dad, Musket and Mr Topsy?' Patrick says. 'You can't save everyone. You shouldn't even be trying.'

'Why are you being so horrible?'

'I'm not, but look at you – you're ill.'

'I'm not ill, I'm frightened.'

'I know that, but why can't you just accept that this isn't good, Lola? It's really, really bad. You can't just fix it. This is it – the end.'

'Maybe it is, but I can still try and . . .' I stop myself. I want to tell him why I'm here, but I can't. He'll tell me I'm crazy and I don't want that. I don't want to fall out with him.

And now it's too late to tell him anyway.

The door slides open again and the panic in my body escalates.

'Okay, you go in first if you want to find Aimee,' Patrick says. 'Let's not argue anymore.' He kisses my forehead. His lips are warm, and linger there for a moment. 'Now just try not to freak out. I know you, Lola – you'll be in meltdown mode before you know it.'

'I'll try. And you stay focused too,' I say, my mouth so dry it's hard to get any words out at all. 'Keep hoping . . . please.'

'I will.'

I give Patrick a tight hug, not wanting to leave him, then I turn and walk slowly towards the door.

'Lola,' Patrick calls. I turn back. 'I . . . I . . .' He shakes his head as if desperately wanting to say something, but can't. 'See you on the other side, mate.'

I wave nervously, step through the doorway and wince at the thud of it closing.

I'm in a room no bigger than a lift. The red glow I'd seen from the outside gently pulsates. It's as if I'm standing inside a living organ.

It's okay, I tell myself, taking in as much air as possible before releasing it through my cracked lips. My legs shake vigorously beneath me and it's taking every ounce of my energy just to stay on my feet.

A few seconds pass and I watch as a thin yellow beam of light, no thicker than a shoelace, emerges from the red haze, twisting towards me. It's mesmerising. I daren't move an inch as it circles my body from my toes up to my head, where it seems to hover and spin for longer, like a golden halo, before it disperses, melting into the warm red air.

Every inch of me tingles, as if I've been wrapped in a warm fluffy towel. But all I can think about is the small blue pot lying in my pocket, like a boil waiting to be popped. What if it's detected? I guess I have to be prepared to take one of the pills quickly if needs be – I can't let them fall into alien hands. Am I brave enough? Don't know.

'STEP ON TO THE BLACK MARKER,' the same electronic voice instructs.

I see a small black circle on the floor in front of me. Swallowing hard, I reluctantly step forwards on to it. Nothing happens. I stand there for a moment, my heartbeat pounding in my eardrums like a tribal anthem. Then a door to my left opens, and the steely voice simply orders, 'GO.'

Chapter Six

I walk into a dark passageway, my head brushing the ceiling and my shoulders rubbing against walls of polished steel. I can just about see my misshapen reflection in the darkness. The horrible saccharine smell is strong, clinging like treacle to the back of my parched throat. I'm suffocating. This is going to be enough to tip me into meltdown. The walls are closing in and I feel like I'm trapped inside a car crusher.

'The walls are not really moving . . . They're not,' I repeat, bending over my knees. 'Stay in control. It's all in your head.'

I have to get a grip and calm down, like Patrick told me to do, or I'll be no use to anyone. I focus on the thought of seeing Dad again.

'Please don't let me lose it, not now.'

My breathing slows a little. This wouldn't be a good place for a panic attack.

At least I'm not dead – that's good. I try not to glimpse my shadowy image too much; I don't like it. And as for where I'm going, I dare not think about that because I'm way too close to passing out as it is.

'PROCEED.'

Just the sound of the electronic voice makes me want to puke again, although I have nothing left to bring up. Crouching, I walk slowly forwards. I'm terrified of what might be inside this dark tunnel with me. My ears strain to hear any identifiable sound, but there's nothing.

Every step is a struggle. I spot brightness up ahead – a small circular opening. It's weird, because I'm definitely scared – no doubt about that – but at the same time I'm curious, excited even. Does that mean I've finally lost the plot?

As I reach the opening, the cold steel walls end, but the tunnel continues on, out into space. It changes to a shimmering glass substance, stretching out, unsupported, over a vast drop into darkness. My tunnel is just one of hundreds forming a huge circle. They're beneath me, above me, all around, like glass tubes of light. I'm not on Earth anymore, that's for sure.

At the end of each glass tube hovers a large white craft. It looks like a plane with no wings. Long, sleek and shiny. More of these ships are gliding below, disappearing into the distance. I stop. The whole scene reminds me of a movie I once saw, set in the future. But this is happening now, in my reality, and it's way beyond anything I could ever have imagined.

'KEEP WALKING,' the voice orders. I'm being watched from somewhere.

I straighten up a little, allowing my feet to take small reluctant steps, as if getting there any slower is going to make a difference. I look through the glass walls and floor to the blackness of space below my feet, hoping I'm not about to plummet to my death.

The glass shimmers in rhythmic waves, and tiny particles of light dance along it like neon sprinkles. I stare out beyond the glass. It's like a docking station or something. But where? Am I in outer space? I can't fathom any of it. But one thing I do know – it's beautiful, majestic.

As I reach the craft, a large door slides open. I'm shaking. Part of me wants to turn and run back up the tunnel, but I know that's not an option. I have to go forwards and face whatever's waiting for me.

I step on to the craft. Inside it's basic and clinical – metal floor and walls, a window on either side. And it's so bright, with white light streaming over us from each end of the craft. Nothing like the darkness of the Leech. A hundred children, maybe more, all different ages and sizes, stare at me. There aren't any seats and it's already full to capacity. I can't see Aimee.

No one talks to me as I squeeze in, but I can hear sobs and frantic whispers. The odd shriek pierces the air, a desperate sound. There are no hand rails, but we're so closely packed we hold each other up. I know I'm going to have to keep calm amongst all these bodies, some of which, like me, are visibly shaking. The door slides shut behind me. Patrick will probably have to catch the next one, I think. I've already decided that these things are like buses, taking us somewhere new.

Slowly the craft pulls away from the glass tunnel, but then immediately drops like a rock in a pond. People scream and try to move, but there's nowhere to go. Finally, to my relief, the craft levels out and glides silently forwards.

The window stretches the length of the craft and I turn and stare out. We are gliding past huge black walls covered in tiny white lights. I can't see where they end. A minute later we're descending again, but much slower this time. Lower and lower we go until we move beneath the black rim of the wall, and my heart almost stops when I see what lies beyond.

Earth, my Earth, is a coloured bauble in the blackness of space, and all around it, like a black ring of iron, are thousands of Leeches. All I can do is press my face to the window and stare.

We never saw any of this from Earth. Once the satellites had been destroyed we only ever saw a thick layer of grey fog through the telescopes. Maybe they have shields that work like one-way mirrors; they can see us, but we can't see them. I look back at the docking station – it's like a huge black barrel with its glass tubes concealed within. I see more white crafts appearing and disappearing beneath its rim as we fly further away.

Hundreds of black Leeches are docked around the barrel's outer edge, delivering their cargo of humans.

There are way more of them than any of us could ever have thought possible. No wonder we can't fight them. I touch the blue pot, but it feels of little use against the enemy laid out before me.

Two small arms then wrap around my waist.

'Aimee!' I hug her tight. 'I can't believe you're here. I didn't see you.'

'I got pushed right over to the back and sat on the floor. Didn't think you were on here either, and then I recognised your school shoes,' she says, still clinging on to me. 'They have a big hole in the toe.'

I smile, and look down at my battered old shoes. 'Knew there'd be a good reason for keeping these grotty old things. Have you seen the view, Aimee?'

'Don't want to.' Her face stays buried in my blazer.

'You can see the ships which brought us here.'

She glances up. 'Where are we going, Lola?'

'I don't know. But I reckon it'll be okay, you'll see.'

'But I just want to go home. I want my mummy.' Her body rocks with deep, painful sobs.

I squeeze her, and a pang of guilt twists inside my chest. If I hadn't let Aimee take Musket for a walk, maybe she would've stayed at home. And I've hardly given my own mum's feelings a single thought. The memory of Dad has been driving me forwards. But Mum will be going out of her mind. Especially after what I said to her before I left.

What if this pushes her over the edge? She's not exactly far from it already. But I know I wouldn't even be here in the first place if she'd let me help Dad, instead of holding me back. No, it's her fault this is happening to me, not mine. She knows how I feel now, and that's a good thing. But I still feel bad – bad that I'll never see her again, bad that I never said goodbye.

The craft stops and then begins edging forwards slowly. A chain of frightened glances whip from person to person, a look of dread in every single face. I stare out of the window again.

A massive silver dome is ahead of us, with ornate black markings and symbols covering its gleaming body. Forming an arch over the dome are three smaller, oval-shaped vessels which hover just above its surface. Below each one, set into the main silver dome, is an indent. I reckon if the smaller vessels were to be lowered into these, they would blend and disappear. These smaller vessels are black with no markings. From a distance they look like a crown across the top of the dome. It's incredible. I blink hard, trying to convince myself the image is real. Suddenly I feel very small and very insignificant.

But we're moving past the regal-looking dome to a cluster of ugly grey ships. Each one is long and slug-like. More are in the distance, sitting behind the ring of Leeches which circles the Earth. We approach one of the ships and enter it through a narrow opening at the side. It's dark inside so I can't see very much, just a few tiny blue lights scattered above.

Our landing is rough, and shakes us as all into a heavy silence.

'Do you think if we ask someone nicely they might take us home later?' Aimee whispers.

'We'll see,' I say, brightly, like my mum used to when I was little.

'Has anyone ever gone home?'

I don't want to lie to her.

'I don't think so, Aimee. But maybe that's because it's so nice here. Maybe people don't want to leave.'

She gives a tentative smile, her dimpled cheeks so sweet. Is it a bad thing to give her hope? I can almost hear Patrick groaning.

The door behind me slides open. I was last in, so I'm first to step out. Aimee is clinging tightly to my hand.

I take a deep breath, but I don't exhale – I can't.

A line of the weirdest creatures I've ever seen is in front of me.

They're about my height, thick set with a curved back like a shell. A wide head sits directly on their bodies, with no sign of a neck. And only one thick leg each seems to be holding them upright. Four tiny black eyes set deep within the coarse olive skin of the creatures have their gaze fixed upon us. And each creature holds something resembling a large hammer, but they look awkward because their hands are really small and dumpy. A row of square grey teeth covered in clear slime lines their mouths. Growls rumble from the backs of their throats. At least thirty of them stand staring at us, poised to attack.

I knew the raiders would probably look different to us – me and Dad had talked about it at length – so I've kind of prepared myself for this moment, if that's possible. I try to hold back on my natural urge to freak out and run. Unfortunately, not everyone is so in control.

A girl to my left begins screaming as soon as she sees them, and it quickly turns into hysteria. A boy tries to calm her down, but it's no use, she's totally lost it.

One of the creatures curls into a ball and rolls towards us, like a giant woodlouse. A large ridge, like an exposed spine, runs all the way down its shell. The creature unfurls in front of the girl, raises its hammer-like weapon and hits her head with one powerful and accurate blow, its arm extending to twice its length before retracting. The girl crumples to the ground.

No one dares to make a sound. The brutal crack of the impact has frightened us into absolute silence.

I can't believe what I've just seen.

By some miracle the girl is still conscious, sobbing into the floor — a line of blood trickling from her forehead into a dark mass by her nose. Another of the creatures rolls forwards and unfurls itself. We all flinch and reach out for each other. The two creatures communicate by deep clicking sounds and then gesture for us to move. The same boy tries to help the girl to her feet, but another ferocious blow knocks him to the ground in a bloody mess.

Aimee is holding my hand so tight it's gone numb. I'm not sure what to think anymore. I don't want to believe they're going to kill us, because that would mean accept-ance, and I'm not ready for that. Maybe the girl screaming had just really annoyed them, because they've let her live. And no doubt they could have killed her in an instant if they'd wanted. What are they going to do with us?

We walk for a long time, flanked on either side by the

creatures, rolling and clicking their jaws, through grey corridor after grey corridor. There isn't much light but the walls look shiny, as if they're coated with something slimy.

I've always hated mazes – they make me panic. And this one feels like a deadly maze, with no way out. Except, when I look up, I notice large circular holes at regular intervals along the top of the walls, like tunnel entrances. Maybe they're ventilation shafts – a possible means of escape, although I have no idea how I'd actually get up there, or worse, where they'd lead me.

But then something moves in one of them. As I stare up, three piercing red eyes shine back at me from the darkness of the tunnel. At least I think they're eyes, because I turn away before the image sinks in.

'Are you all right, Lola?' Aimee asks. 'You're hurting my hand.'

I probably look like a ghost.

'Um, fine . . .' I say. 'I'm sorry.'

'You said it would be okay.'

I look back, but we're way past the tunnel entrance now. 'Yeah, I did, didn't I?'

I shake my head. It was probably nothing, my mind playing tricks on me. Are they messing with our thoughts again? Like that boy said? But I don't have a headache.

We pass a line of four rooms on the left of us, but I can't see inside, they're closed off with heavy metal doors. Finally we arrive at a huge carved panel at the end of the corridor. It's black, and three times as tall as me. I'm feeling exposed at the front of the crowd, vulnerable. A cold shiver sweeps down my spine. I have a horrible feeling that something bad is lying behind that panel.

One of the creatures waves his podgy palm over a small white light situated in the centre. The panel slowly opens, sliding down into the ground.

Pushed from all directions by the creatures' hammers, we have no choice but to go in. It's a gigantic room with pale grey walls and a rough metal floor. I blink twice, and then again, because I can't quite believe what I see stretching out before me.

Cages.

Huge cages fill the room — three storeys high and four abreast with alleyways and stairs running between them. They go back further than I can see. And every one is jammed full of people.

And yet, even with so many people, the air is eerily quiet and still — heavy with fear and sweat.

We're pushed again, this time towards the far left of the room. More strange creatures wait for us, but not the weird, clicking, rolling ones. These are more like humans. Well, apart from their red skin and dark blue hair.

They are dressed in brightly coloured uniforms. One, a female with hair that nearly reaches the floor, steps forwards. Something like a smile skips across her red lips.

'Welcome, newcomers. Do not be alarmed. I am a Malion, a species similar to your own. It is our job to take care of you during your stay with us.' Her voice is high and crisp, and her words sound rehearsed. 'You will form a line in front of me and I will give each of you a bowl. You are then to go and stand by the Malion with the corresponding coloured uniform.'

It is only then that I see the bars of each cage are painted a different colour: yellow, orange, white, red, blue and green. They are all the colours I can see, but there could be more out of sight.

I swallow hard, my mouth lacking any hint of moisture. What I wouldn't do right now for a bottle of cold water. I look at the massive cages and the blank faces staring back at me through the bars. Some cages hold children as young as three or four. In the cage closest to me, a boy about my age is staring out.

All the children's eyes are vacant, their faces grubby, and they're all clutching small coloured bowls. It's a pitiful sight. I try to think of a reason, an explanation to make sense of what I'm seeing, but all I can come up with is one word – prison.

A queue forms and I find myself at the front of it. Aimee nestles into me, refusing to surrender the grip she has on my hand. The woman with the long hair beckons Aimee forwards, but Aimee only hugs me tighter, her hold firm and determined.

A male Malion joins the female. He is tall and wide, with short spiked hair and a black uniform. He says nothing, but stands with his arms behind his back. The other Malions seem to respond immediately to his presence and stand a little straighter. His eyes rest on me and Aimee. I look away from him. There is something unsettling about his gaze.

'Come, girl . . . I will not hurt you,' the woman says, still speaking awkwardly, as if her words are chosen carefully.

'Go on, Aimee,' I say, kissing the top of her head. 'We have to.'

She looks up at me and nods. 'Okay, but don't leave me, Lola.'

This time I hear Patrick's voice in my head: *Don't promise her anything.* I just nod.

The woman holds a small device which looks like a pen. She presses it to Aimee's temple. I look on, fighting an overwhelming need to protect her. But I hold back and when the device is removed Aimee seems to be okay, even managing a faint smile when she looks back at me.

'Give me your arm,' the Malion orders, then adds, 'Forgive me, I should have said "please".'

Aimee lifts her arm and the Malion takes hold of her hand, shoving her sleeve up to her elbow. Aimee's wrist is placed through a metal ring like a clamp, which is then squeezed down on to her flesh. I want to go to her again, but stop myself. Aimee flinches as the clamp is released to show a band of yellow dye, the skin around it red and inflamed. She's given a small yellow bowl and guided towards a Malion with the yellow uniform.

It's my turn and my stomach is doing somersaults. The male Malion is still watching me. I think he might be in charge.

The pen-like device feels cold on my temple and I can hear its gentle humming.

'What is that thing?' I ask.

The woman looks at me. Her eyes are like black marble. But she can't quite hide the look of annoyance that my question has caused. Maybe she's not as tolerant as she's trying to appear.

'I'm scanning you,' she replies.

I must look surprised, because I didn't actually expect her to answer me.

'Scanning for what?'

But now she just scowls and says nothing. I've probably pushed my luck too far. She pushes my sleeve up and lowers the clamp down on to my wrist. It hurts and burns in equal amounts, and I'm left with a vivid blue ring imprinted into my skin, like a tattooed band. I don't register the colour at first, but then she turns and places a small blue bowl in my hand, and points to the Malion to her left.

'N-no,' I say. 'There's been a mistake. I need to be with Aimee. I need a yellow bowl.'

The woman shakes her head and merely points again.

'No, I won't be separated from her,' I insist.

Aimee starts crying and tries to run to me, but the Malion she's with holds her back.

'Get your hands off her,' I scream, and shove the blue bowl back at the Malion. 'I need a yellow one . . . please.'

But she merely stares over my shoulder. And the male Malion is smiling. Why is he smiling?

I hear a clicking noise behind me and turn to see one of the rolling creatures.

Then I see a hammer. And then I see nothing.

Chapter Seven

The taste of blood in my mouth registers before anything else, then the physical pain of my head throbbing, followed by the fact that my face seems to be kissing the floor. Slowly, and aware that I'm groaning loudly, I open my eyes. My vision is blurred, but after a few forceful blinks, I know exactly where I am.

My bum is pressed hard against metal bars and every other part of me has someone else's body part touching it. I'm in a cage.

I manage to sit up, my head spinning. It's so crowded that I only have a tiny space to sit in. The blue bowl is propped up against my leg.

A girl about my age, with long, greasy blonde hair, frowns and points to it. 'That's yours, that is,' she says.

I shove it away from me. 'Thanks, but I don't want it.'

'You have to have it,' she says. 'You okay?' She flicks a finger in the direction of my forehead.

I wince as I touch a large, smooth lump protruding from my skin. 'Ouch,' I groan. My tongue also finds a small cut on my bottom lip which explains the taste of blood. I sit for a second trying to think, and then I remember.

'Aimee . . . I have to find her.' I grab the bars and pull myself up, my head swimming, my legs wobbly. 'Where did they take her?' The girl looks at me, confused by my sudden surge of energy. 'There was a girl, red hair, about seven years old . . .'

But the girl just shrugs, seemingly uninterested. 'Probably in a different cage. What colour bowl did she have?'

'Yellow.'

'She'll be up top then. Lightweights up there.' She looks up and I follow her gaze. I remember seeing other cages above. Our ceiling must be their floor.

'Can I get up there?'

The girl sniggers. 'Oh yeah, course you can. Have a cup of tea while you're up there and say hi to everyone for me.'

'No need to be sarky,' I snap.

She shrugs again. I look out over the sea of heads and bodies, all clutching their little blue bowls. The cages go back so far I can't see where they end, it's too dark. Some faces stare back.

'What the hell is this place?' I ask, collapsing back down and almost flattening the poor boy next to me. I try and apologise. I'm so thankful I'm near the edge and not stuck somewhere in the middle.

The girl shakes her head. 'You just said it. Welcome to hell.'

'What's that supposed to mean?'

'Exactly what I said, unless you can think of a better name for it.'

'I'm looking for my dad, and my dog, too. I know it's a long shot, but do you know what might have happened to them or how I can find them?'

She sniggers then lowers her eyes to fiddle with her frayed shoelace. I'm quickly coming to the conclusion that I don't like this girl much.

'Did you hear me?' I say.

'Yeah, I heard ya.'

'Well?'

'Who knows? But if I was you, I'd accept the fact that you won't be seeing them again. I gave up on that months ago.'

'Months? How long have you been in here?' I ask, only now noticing how deathly pale she looks. Her features are hard, and made worse by the lack of flesh on them.

'A while. Don't eat the food, that's my advice. Those there are water fountains.' She points to long tubes hanging down from the ceiling. I see someone stand up, pull a ring underneath the tube and then suck from one of the prongs which jut out from it. 'You should drink plenty; it gets really hot in here.' She lowers her voice. 'But people stay around longer if they don't eat the food.'

'Why would you want to stay here longer?' My plan is

to get out as quick as I can. 'So you're saying people do leave?'

'Yeah, but I reckon when you leave it's permanent, like *the elimination of your existence*,' she says, imitating the electronic voice I'd heard earlier.

I know this situation is dire, but I have to stay open-minded, for Dad's sake as well as Musket and Aimee's. And then there's Patrick – where is he? Has he been given a bowl and a cage too? I hope he's safe.

I stand up again and shout as loud as I can. 'Aimee! Patrick! Can you hear me?'

No reply. Everyone glares at me again, and a female Malion in a blue uniform marches to my side of the cage.

'Sit down and be quiet,' she barks. In her hand is a long metal rod, pulsating with an ominous red glow. 'Or I'll punish you.'

'Please. . . W-what's going to happen to us?'

The Malion bares her sharp blue teeth at me and growls. Did she really say we were a similar species? She shoves the rod through the bars, the point only milli-metres from my face. I freeze. I can feel a burning heat on my flesh. One touch and it'll scorch me, I'm sure of it. The Malion's pale red skin is flawless. Her dark blue hair swept into a ponytail of intricate weaves. She leans in, and I can smell her stale breath.

'You are to be fed,' she says with a snarl, then stalks away.

The lights brighten slightly and everyone sits up a little straighter. The girl I've been speaking to yanks me to the floor.

'You don't wanna be messin' with the guards, giving them an excuse to beat us up. Don't ask no questions.'

'Okay,' I say. 'I'm sorry.'

'You need to learn fast in this place, got it? Or we all get punished.'

I nod again. She's right; the last thing I need to do is draw the wrong type of attention to myself.

'So . . . what did she mean, about being fed?'

'It happens about ten times a day — plus snack times now and again.'

'Right,' I say.

'You'll need your bowl too. But like I said before, try not to eat much. The food here is like a drug, you get hooked. See all their faces? They're desperate for it, addicted. I'm Evie, by the way.' She stretches out a bony hand towards me.

'Lola.' I smile cautiously, feeling obliged to return her gesture. 'So we get food now?'

Evie nods.

Can that really be as bad as she makes it sound? I need to keep my strength up. I need to eat because who knows what's coming? I also want to shout for Aimee again, but the Malion is still hovering nearby, so I'll have to try later.

The lights get even brighter and I can see everyone more clearly. The prisoners do look desperate, excited even. But maybe that's just because they're really hungry. But their manic faces aren't the only thing I can see. Everyone is dirty, I'd noticed that before, but some of them are wearing clothes which are torn like rags and blackened as if burned.

An alarm rings out and everyone stands up and starts shuffling forwards. I have no choice but to join them, getting swept along in the frantic tide of sweaty bodies.

'There are hatches at the front,' Evie says, shouting through a gap as she gets shunted further away from me. She jabs a finger in the direction I need to go.

I am buffeted hard from all angles, can hardly breathe as I'm squashed and squeezed, the smell of sweat stinging my senses. My heart is seriously racing now, my claustrophobia hitting me like a giant boulder – not good. I want to, no, I *need* to get out of here. My ears burn as dizziness blurs my sight and I feel like I'm going to faint, I know it, but still I'm pushed forwards.

I'm panicking . . . Going . . .

I must have lost consciousness for a minute or two and probably only stayed upright due to the closeness of the other bodies around me, because suddenly my nose bashes against something hard and my eyes shoot open to a haze of blue, which slowly morphs back into a row of bars.

Someone is standing on the other side of them. I screw my face up and shake my head. My nose is killing me, throbbing as if it's twice the size it should be.

'Hurry up,' a voice says from behind, prodding me painfully in the ribs. I then realise I'm already at the hatch. It's just a square opening cut into the bars with a solid door that slides across.

'Your bowl,' a voice says.

I slowly look up, and I think my jaw drops again, just as it did the first time I saw those fiery eyes. It's the boy, but now he's wearing blue trousers and a short-sleeved shirt. A uniform. He's a guard.

He stares back at me too, mouth open, looking just as shocked. But then something else passes over his face. I can't read it. 'Your bowl,' he repeats, but less fiercely this time. His English is perfect, like the Malions'.

'Um, y-yeah . . . Here,' I say, and hand him my bowl through the gap in the bars. I wince as a severe pain shoots down my nose, causing tears to flood my eyes.

He flashes me a look and then quickly lowers his gaze to my bowl as he scans the bottom of it across a smooth panel on a trolley beside him. Then he scoops in a ladle of thick brown gloop. He fills the bowl to the brim and gives it back to me. I notice he's wearing a large black-and-silver ring, a smooth cabochon which looks like a beetle clinging to his finger.

'Thanks . . . Is there a-a spoon?' I ask.

He shakes his head.

'You eat it with your fingers,' a girl beside me snipes. I think it's the same girl who just prodded me. 'Now get out of the way. We'll be here all day at this rate and I *need* my food.'

'Wait,' the boy snaps.

I look up at him, and without my permission, I feel my cheeks flush. He points to my nose. I touch it and a layer of warm blood coats the tips of my fingers.

'Oh.'

He hands me a small piece of cloth. 'Please sit down, before you fall down,' he says, ordering me, not telling me.

I nod and manage a smile, but he doesn't respond to it. 'Next,' he calls, looking away.

I make my way back to the edge of the cage, amazed I'm staying on my feet and thankful that my place is still there. Evie isn't back yet. I think she headed towards a different hatch. The brown gloop in my bowl smells horrible, like it's gone off or something. But my mind isn't on the food.

I can't believe I've just seen him again, the boy who saved me and Mum. He's one of them. I knew deep down he had to be. Nobody has eyes like that, not if they're human. He's not one of those Malions – not with his pale skin and dark hair – but he's still my enemy, my captor. Yet he saved me. It doesn't make sense.

The piece of cloth is now soaked in blood, but at least my nose has finally stopped bleeding. I shove the cloth into my trouser pocket and try hard to get his face out of my head. I need a distraction. Tentatively I dip my fingers into the bowl and scoop a little of the mixture into my mouth. Actually, it tastes better than it smells. The texture is greasy and the lumps of meat are chewy – at least, I think they're lumps of meat – but the sauce is no worse than Mum's gravy. In fact, if I'm honest, it tastes better than some of the stuff Mum created with our rations.

I have a sudden memory of Mum trying to cook something edible with a tin of corn beef, dried egg powder, rehydrated chicken tikka and pineapple chunks. I'd wished her luck.

I don't know what Evie meant about getting hooked on this stuff, but I'll have to take the risk. I have to eat.

'Go easy,' Evie says as she arrives back, squeezing into a tiny space beside me, causing a groan to ripple around us as others have to readjust their positions.

'Why? It's not that bad, and I'm hungry.'

'Trust me. I've seen what happens to people who eat too much in this place.'

'The boy who served me the food, do you know who he is?'

Evie looks over to the hatch. 'Dunno.'

'He looks a bit human. I didn't imagine them like that.'

'Well, the workers are not the real problem.'

'What do you mean?'

She beckons me forwards. Her breath stinks too. 'The Malions, your human boy lookalike, and them rolling things – which are called Kal – just work here. They're not controlling these ships.'

'How do you know that?'

'I used to be in the red cages. The Malion there talked more, not like the misery guts we've got now. Anyway, she told me that the creatures in control are called Arlatans. She said they're monsters. They visit the cages sometimes. I've never seen one, but sometimes, at night, when the lights are out, I've seen things sort of slithering across the bars. I think that's them. Someone always disappears when that happens – and they don't come back.'

'So what do you think happens to them?'

She shrugs. 'I don't reckon it's good.'

I had a feeling she'd say that, but her words still make me shiver.

Everyone is now scooping up their food as if competing

for Olympic gold in being gross.

'They're all enjoying it,' I say.

'Well, they're all idiots. Like I said, the more you eat, the more you want,' Evie says, picking the tiniest piece out of her bowl and popping it into her mouth – grimacing and forcing herself to chew as if it's laced with poison or something. A slight overreaction, I think.

I take another scoop of the food. I'm suddenly hungrier than I first thought, and even if Evie is prepared to starve herself to death, I'm not. I need to eat. I need to find my dad and Musket. Then we can help Patrick and Aimee. And Evie. My list is getting longer.

'I'll take my chances,' I say, and begin shovelling down the gloop along with the rest of them.

Chapter Eight

The reason everyone eats so fast soon becomes apparent when small machines glide into the cage from the hatches. About the size of a microwave oven, they hover in the air, travelling from person to person.

'What are those?' I ask.

'Dishwashers,' Evie replies. 'They never give you enough time to eat though. Not that it bothers me, of course,' she shrugs. 'When they come to you just put your bowl in the compartment. Each bowl has a number on the bottom – probably some fancy electronic chip or something.' She lifts her bowl up high and points to the base, but I don't see anything on it. 'They scan it for your code. The machine then empties out any leftover food and cleans it. But it also records how much you've eaten.'

I look at Evie's bowl, which is still half full. 'What do they do about you?'

She looks over her shoulder, as if checking the guards are out of earshot. 'Drag me in for an examination every now and again. Hurt me a bit with those rods they carry. The Malions like that part – enjoy it a bit too much, if you ask me.' She pulls back her sleeve and I gasp. Above the blue and red tattooed bands on her wrist are areas of circular, blistered and scared skin.

'Did they do that to you?' I say, trying not to sound shocked.

'Yeah, got them all over. I'm like a dot-to-dot picture, me. Sometimes they're impatient and just burn right through your clothes, which melts the fabric into your skin. That's really bad.'

'And you still refuse to eat?' I say, shaking my head in disbelief.

'Physical pain I can handle, but they ain't controlling me. I eat when I want to, not because I have to,' she says lowering her sleeve again.

I remember the rod, how close I'd come to bearing an identical burn on my cheek. I look around, at the burned clothing and scorch marks. Many other prisoners have obviously suffered the same fate, for whatever reason.

'Besides, sometimes I empty a bit into other people's bowls, to fool 'em.' She nods to the empty one on my lap. 'Cheat the system a bit.'

I frown, but before I can answer her, someone speaks.

'She doesn't want to cheat the system.'

The boy is kneeling down by the cage. His expression

still unreadable as he stares at my battered face. 'I've come to check on your injuries. You had a nose bleed, and I see that you also have a head wound.'

'Yes, but I'm fine now,' I say, thrown by his sudden appearance.

'I'll be the judge of that. Stand up, please.'

I pull myself up, using the bars for support. I'm still reeling from seeing Evie's scars. 'What's going to happen to us?' I ask.

He doesn't answer. He has one of the pen-like scanners in his hand.

'Because I need to find my dad, and my dog. And then there are the people I came in here with. I don't know how to find them.'

'Lola . . .' Evie tugs at my trouser leg. I look down, her glare speaks volumes. I press my lips together, suddenly aware that I need to be careful what I say. I can see one of the rods attached to his belt.

'I need to scan you again.' He puts his hand through the bars and presses the device to my temple. I can see his ring more clearly now; it's beautiful, black with tiny silver markings all over it. Three thick silver shanks attach it to his finger like a claw.

The scanner is cold. 'The Kal did that with their hammer,' I say, when I see him inspecting the large bump below my fringe.

'The hammers are called ballams,' he corrects.

'Oh, right – okay. I'll try and remember that next time I come face to face with one,' I say, a little more aggressively than I intended.

Again, he doesn't respond and I feel angry with myself. I need to stay calm and composed if I'm to get my answers.

'You feeling all right?' he asks, removing the scanner and reading something on it. 'Your results are very high. You are anxious.'

Is he seriously surprised that I'm anxious? 'So would you be if you thought you were about to die. Is that what's going to happen to me?'

His orange eyes flicker to an even deeper shade, and his skin appears paler, ashen. It's obvious he can't, or doesn't want to, answer my question.

'I'll take that as a yes then.'

'It's not my place to say anything,' he replies.

'Of course it isn't,' I say.

Others are looking at us now, including the Malion guards. I can hear their whispers.

'So you're one of them, then?' I ask. 'But that doesn't make any sense . . . Why did you . . . Why did you help me and my mum last night?'

He looks apprehensive. Sucking in his bottom lip. 'I do not know.'

'Oh, right . . .' That's not the answer I was expecting. 'So what then? You just felt sorry for me or something?'

'I said I do not know.'

I'm confused, or maybe I'm missing something. 'You were on the common today too – I saw you.'

'Yes.' His chin lifts and he looks directly at me. 'You ran towards it,' he says, shaking his head. 'Directly into the ship's path. Did you want to get taken?'

I remember the look I'd seen on his face, how my actions must have seemed to him. 'Yes.'

'Explain,' he asks.

'You think I'm crazy.'

'To do what I saw you do . . . yes.'

'Why were you there?' I ask.

He stares around the room as if looking for someone. 'We visit the surface occasionally. We're sent down to do a micro-scan of the area before a raid. Checking for anything unusual.'

'Oh.' Mum was right then; they have been walking amongst us. But if he can go to the surface, maybe he can help me.

'So what's your name?' I ask.

'Torrin.'

'I'm Lola.'

He nods, but looks away again. 'I don't need to know your name,' he says.

'Okay.'

I want to bombard him with questions, about him, about this place, about their plans for Earth. But I have a feeling my time is running out. I can sense he's about to leave. I edge nearer to the bars.

'Torrin, will you help me find my dad? He was taken yesterday. And the two people I came in here with. I know the girl, Aimee, is in the yellow cages. But my friend Patrick, he's my age and I've not seen him since that processing place. I have to find them.' I take a deep breath. 'And then there's my dog,' I continue. 'He got taken just before me. You must have seen him. He's a black Labrador and he's wearing a red collar with his name on. His name's Musket.'

I stop talking and bite my lip, not wanting to babble on, but Torrin doesn't fill the silence with the answers I desperately want to hear.

'Musket never ended up in the same place that I did. Why?' I ask, trying to prompt him to speak.

'He wouldn't have,' he finally says, his words so quiet I have to press my face to the bars just to hear. 'Animals get taken to a different ship.'

'Can you go there, maybe look for him for me?' I ask, trying not to sound too manic in case I frighten him off. 'He'll come if you call his name.'

Torrin looks at me. One of my hands is gripping the bars and he places his palm on top. I go to draw my hand away but he tightens his grip. His palm is rough – a worker's hand. I'm nervous, but I don't think I'm scared of him. 'They don't normally keep the animals alive for very long.'

'What do you mean . . . They kill them?' My heart falters and my breathing deepens. T-tell me . . . Please.'

'They use the animals they capture to . . .' I can sense he doesn't want to say it, but I nod, urging him to carry on. 'To feed all the humans they have imprisoned here.'

He gives a swift glance toward my bowl on the floor. I can't breathe or swallow. 'T-the food,' I splutter. 'You mean that c-could've been Musket?' My stomach heaves at the memory of those chewy lumps of meat in my mouth.

'That wouldn't have been your dog, he only got captured today. It takes time to . . .'

'Prepare him, you mean. Oh, well, that's all right then. Might just be tomorrow or the next day,' I cry. Tears stream down my cheeks. 'Please go and find him, you know where he'll be,' I beg. 'I c-can't lose him too.'

'It's too late.'

'Please, try.'

'I can't do that.' His voice is blunt, final.

'Why?'

'Stop, don't ask me to.' His face tenses and his eyes burn like an inferno.

I yank my hand away; I can't bear him to touch me. But I have to think quickly. 'My dad, then, do you know what's happened to him?'

'I have to go.'

'Please, Torrin. I have to find him. It's why I ran towards the ship. And my friends . . .' I reach through the bars and grab hold of his shirt. He throws me a look which makes my breath catch – rage clinging to every strained muscle of his face.

I must never trust this creature.

I loosen my grip. He walks away without a glance. My cheeks press hard against the smooth surface of the bars, as if trying to squeeze between them. But all I can do is watch as he walks towards the door and disappears through it.

My performance hasn't gone unnoticed. The male Malion from earlier is standing at the side of room, his arms folded. His expression is stern, unwavering. I have a feeling I've made a big mistake drawing his attention for a second time.

I slump back to the floor. 'You idiot, Lola,' I hiss under my breath.

'Bit harsh,' Evie says.

'I said too much, didn't I?'

She shrugs. 'Maybe. Brave or stupid, you're definitely one of the two.'

'Who is that?' I say nodding towards the male Malion.

'His name is Jaxz. He's in charge of the guards. You think the females are cruel. I've seen him punish people and they can't walk for days after. You don't want to be getting on the wrong side of him.'

'I'll try and remember that,' I say.

The bowl-washing machine has made it to us. I feel sick as I place my bowl in the compartment. The thought of what might be happening to Musket makes me want to scream. 'Did you know we were eating the animals? The animals they take?'

Evie laughs. 'Oh no, you're not a veggie, are you?'

'No, but my dog got taken.' I press my fingers to my eyes, trying to stop the flow of tears from coming again. 'I'm not eating another thing in this grotty place . . . ever.'

'Well, I did say that,' Evie says, shuffling beside me, trying to make more space for herself. 'Although, not necessarily for those reasons. Rotten luck about your dog though, but at least he'll be put to good use – keeping us lot alive an' all.'

'I'm guessing you've never owned a dog.'

'Allergic.'

'Figures.'

'Meat is meat. Can't pick and choose. Had this friend

once would only eat ugly animals. Flaky or what?' she says.

'But it's my dog!'

Evie doesn't reply. This is getting worse. I still have no idea where to find Dad or Patrick, how to get to Aimee, or even if I'm going to die in this cage. But I do know one thing for sure. That boy helped me once. He's got to help me again. He's my only chance, my only hope of escape. I have to get him back.

Chapter Nine

The room darkens even more and we're told, very bluntly, to sleep. No blankets or pillows, just each other's bodies to lean on. I'm resting my head on someone's thigh and Evie is leaning against my back. I literally cannot move.

I tried to wash earlier beneath one of the water prongs. It wasn't easy; the water just a pathetic trickle. There is no privacy, so I washed my face and armpits the best I could. The toilets are in the middle of the cage, just a row of holes in the ground. I try to avoid going until I'm desperate. It stinks. I stink.

But being sweaty is the least of my worries. Fighting my fear of enclosed spaces is proving way more difficult to cope with. The suffocating darkness doesn't help either,

80

or my body being shoved hard up against the outer bars of the cage. I can feel my skin bruising with every movement I make. The bump on my head continues to throb, made worse by lying down. At least my cut lip is starting to heal.

I stare through the bars to focus on what little bit of open space there is beyond them. Another cage sits the other side of the walkway with green bars enclosing its victims. The hazy light makes it impossible to see individuals in the ocean of sleeping bodies. I try to think of a possible reason for the different coloured bars – I can't.

It isn't silent. Somewhere nearby, someone is crying. Their sobs are muffled, as if they do not want to be heard. Maybe a louder show of distress would result in punishment. I remember Evie's burns and the heat of that red-hot stick near my face. It scares me. I wish I wasn't here. I wish I was in a nightmare; at least then I'd get to wake up.

A movement catches my eye, above the cages, high up on the wall. Is it one of the monsters? It's moving slowly around the walls, getting closer. I try and blink it away. Maybe I'm hallucinating. But then three red lights shine through the darkness . . . No, not lights, *eyes*. Like those I saw before, in the hole in the corridor wall.

It's on the side of the green cage now, a huge mound of something. A Malion is dragging someone out of the green cage. I can hear them whimpering, as if they're clinging to the last breaths of life. Something is happening, but I can't see what. Scuffling, and I can hear a strange cracking sound. The mound is moving away again. The prisoner is nowhere to be seen.

I turn away and curl up into a ball, not daring to look again. It wasn't real. What I think I saw, it wasn't real.

I must have drifted off, because I wake a little while later. My stomach is grumbling, but how can I be hungry? How can I possibly want to face the food after finding out where it comes from? But I do – I want their food. I close my eyes again, trying to find some comfort away from my mad thoughts, my desperate hunger. But sleep isn't going to come easy second time round. I need to either find a way out, or just sit, wait and accept that I've failed. And I'm not prepared to do that – not yet, not *ever*.

My hand touches the blue pot that is still safely concealed in my blazer pocket. I remember my dad when he first told me they were going to develop a weapon that could end the war. I can see his face now. My dad has a happy face. Even when he's sad his features refuse to be miserable. But that day he was more than happy, he was full of hope.

He never told me what they were working on, and I tried not to ask him too much. But I think I imagined it to be a beast of a weapon capable of blowing our attackers out of the sky and back to where they came from. But I was wrong. Project Sapphire. Is Patrick right about these pills? Are they really weapons? I try and shake away my doubts.

I must have fallen asleep again because the next thing I hear and see is screeching alarms and the glare of bright lights. Loud bellowing and terrifying screams make me sit bolt upright. My hand is still clasping the blue pot.

'What's happening?' I cry, trying to blink the sleep from my eyes and focus on the mass of scrambling bodies around me.

'Some of the greens are leaving,' Evie says, and I can hear the tremble in her voice.

I look across at the huge cage beside ours, reminded of what I saw last night. Inside, some of the people are lined up and being led out. A Malion is standing at the cage door waving a small white cube under each of the prisoners' noses as they pass. They immediately stop crying, as if an off switch has been pushed.

'Drugging them,' Evie says. 'Controlling them.'

I watch as one boy resists and tries to stay in the cage. The Malion beats him to the ground with the metal rod. His desperate screams make me cover my ears. I'm pushed from behind by others wanting to take a closer look. Each green is having their wrist tattooed again with the clamp.

'Where are they taking them?'

'Dunno, but what I do know is that's the last cage people are moved to. And do you notice anything different about the prisoners in it?'

I'm hard up against the bars, trying to elbow myself some space. 'They look bigger,' I say, noticing this for the first time. Some are even verging on the obese.

'Fat, you mean, and there are no little kids either,' Evie observes, lifting her eyebrows, just like Mum does when she thinks something's a bit iffy. 'That's why I don't eat anything in this place. I have a theory, you see. When you reach a certain weight they take you somewhere else.'

'Maybe that's a good thing, maybe they think bigger is

healthier or something.'

'Yeah right, whatever. All I know is there are six different coloured cages in this room. Tiny kids go in white, then on to yellow, red, blue, orange and green. You progress through the colours until you're in the last cage. *That* cage. They feed you all the time. You're hungry all the time, and then you get fatter. It does my head in big time, Lola. But at least I know if I stay in here, I stay alive. I am not going to be a green.'

'But why would they spend time waiting for us to grow just to kill us off? This might not be as bad as it looks.'

'Then you're an idiot, Miss Lola Loser.'

I watch as the prisoners are led away, I count at least thirty. But I don't want to think about the greens anymore, or where they might be going. Instead I turn my attention to not spending another night in this hell hole.

'Evie, how can I get out of here? Seriously. I mean, people must be taken out for things.'

'Why would you want to leave? You might not come back,' she says, her eyes big and fearful.

'I don't want to come back,' I say. 'What if I pretend to be ill?'

Evie shakes her head. 'They'll scan you. They can tell in an instant if you're healthy or not. That's why they scan you before you come in. That's why that boy came back to check on you.'

'Then what about if I cause a commotion? Start yelling my head off or pick a fight?'

'It's happened a few times. If it's serious, you'll get

dragged out and probably killed. If it's just a scuffle then you'll stay in here to be beaten and scorched by the Malions. I wouldn't recommend either.'

'How do you know they get killed?'

'I don't, but they never come back. Your best bet is your admirer.'

'My what?' I say.

'The boy that seems so concerned about your health. I reckon he could get you out of here for a while if you asked him.'

'Torrin? You mean I should be nice to him?'

Evie rolls her eyes. 'I think you need to be a bit more than nice.'

I'm not sure I could persuade a human that I liked him, let alone an alien. 'I can't flirt.'

'You asked me for my advice and that's it. And now's your chance.'

The food alarm rings out and the lights brighten. The serving hatches are opened and I see Torrin standing at the same hatch as last night. Butterflies invade my stomach and a cold wave ripples through me. Everyone moves forwards. I'm tempted to go to another hatch, give myself more time to think, but that would mean pushing into the middle of the crowd and I'm anxious enough just being by the edge.

I shuffle forwards with everyone, trying to stop a repeat of yesterday's panic attack. I hate the fact that I'm hungry, and the thought of what I'll be given to eat makes me want to sit down again. But I have to keep strong.

It takes a while to reach the hatch. The whole time I'm

preparing my first sentence. Not too direct – there are too many ears listening. I nervously fidget with my school tie, twisting it around my fingers. He'll see right through me, I know it. But I needn't have bothered with all my pre-planning; this time he doesn't react at all when he sees me. In fact, he seems unwilling to even look at me.

'Bowl,' he says, blank – cold.

His harshness makes tears prick at the corners of my eyes. I don't know why I feel so hurt, but I do. Maybe because he's my only hope of getting to Dad, and that hope is slipping away. He hands back my bowl. I stare helplessly at the gloop slopping at the brim.

'I c-can't eat this.' I say. 'Is there anything else?'

'No.'

'B-but please . . .'

I then get shoved violently to one side by a boy trying to get to the front. I cry out as my already aching body slams into someone else, forcing the air from my lungs. I catch sight of Torrin staring at me. But he turns his head away before I can read his expression. He doesn't speak to me. If he cared he would speak to me, wouldn't he?

I stagger back to my place, clutching my chest. I sit, unable to make myself eat, but watching others devour their food with such enthusiasm is making it harder to resist.

Why do I want this food so badly?

I keep thinking of what Evie said, about getting hooked. The food is like a drug. It's only the thought of Musket that's stopping me from diving in. The smell which I found disgusting before is now so mouth-watering.

Evie is back and slumps down beside me. She seems pleased that I'm not eating anything, as if she knows I've taken her advice or something.

'They put something in the food, don't they?' I ask.

'I think so. It's the only reason I can come up with. But if you only eat a little then it doesn't seem to affect you too much.'

I cover my nose and push the bowl as far away as I can, which isn't very far at all. A boy next to me is staring at it, his empty one on his lap.

'Have it, if you want,' I say.

He dithers, as if battling with his conscience. I push it a little closer to him, but Evie grabs my arm. 'What the hell are you doing?'

'I was just . . .'

The boy grabs it, but it falls from his hand. Something stabs into his arm and then into mine. Two Malions are standing beside the cage, jamming their rods deep into our limbs. The point has gone through my school uniform and pierced my skin like a hook. Now it's burning through my blazer and into my flesh. I cry out. Smoke fills the air and the smell of burning invades my nose. I try to get away, and look up to see tears rolling down Evie's face as she watches my punishment.

I can't get my breath. 'Please . . . s-stop,' I cry. Everything is blurring, swaying. I ball my hands into fists and try to scream out the pain. I never thought anything could hurt so much. I sob as the rod is released.

The Malion called Jaxz appears beside the cage and bends down to my height. His skin is rough, his eyes black. 'You do not share your food with anyone. Eat what we provide or my guards will punish you again. Understand?'

I nod, my breath juddering as I do so.

He leaves and the two Malions follow. The boy is in a crumpled, shivering heap by my feet. I feel terrible. It's my fault he got punished. I was so stupid.

'I'm sorry,' I say, but he ignores me. My hand presses down over my wound, which continues to burn beneath my palm.

'Get up,' Evie whispers. 'Get it under water.'

She pulls me to my feet and I let out another cry as her action stretches the skin around the burn.

Torrin is still at the hatch. There isn't a glimmer of concern on his face. I was wrong about him; he'll never help me.

I'm on my own.

Chapter Ten

The minutes feel like hours, every one of them a torturous wait. I haven't dared look at my arm yet, but the constant face-pulling from Evie tells me it's not a pretty sight. She keeps informing me that it's not good to get burned through your clothing – as if I had much choice in the matter. They didn't exactly ask me to roll up my sleeve. The water did little to help. It only dribbles from the tubes and isn't even cold.

The pain is nauseating, unbearable. But apparently I don't have to worry about infection; they'll give me medicine if that happens. But according to Evie the pain and the scarring are both part of the punishment. So they're keeping us alive for something. Maybe Torrin will come back and check on me again. Is that his job? A kind of medic?

To take my mind off the pain, I try to take in my surroundings. Standing like guards by the door where we came in are two of the rolling creatures – the Kal. At least three Malions for each cage patrol up and down every few minutes, barking at people to be quiet. I see no one else. I also witness two more people getting burned. The Malions are vicious. Torrin is nowhere to be seen.

Meal times come and go, but I continue to eat nothing. I know I'm risking further punishment, but at least my weird craving for their food is easing.

I'm worried about Evie. Her eyes are bloodshot with dark rings etched around them, and her skin is pasty white beneath the smears of muck. It frightens me to see how bad she looks – much worse than yesterday.

'You need to eat more, Evie. You're not going to get fat by eating one bowlful.' I'd rather she became addicted to their food than died.

'I s'pose I should.'

I know Evie has managed well so far, eating enough to keep her alive but never getting hooked. But I reckon her spirit is dying now, and that's much more terrifying to watch.

Although the effort it takes to get served every meal-time is hardly worth it when all we get for it is a bowlful of thick brown gloop. When the dishwashing machine comes round, neither of us has ever eaten very much. I force a little of it down out of necessity, being careful not to have too much. I feel a hypocrite, telling Evie to eat when I can't even look at the lumps of meat without thinking of Musket. I miss him. I miss his chocolate brown eyes, the silky feel of his fur. I'd tell him everything, and I knew he understood. But I know I'll never see him again.

'I'll probably be called in for an examination again soon,' Evie says.

'Then you should eat more, to keep them off your back,' I insist.

She shrugs her bony shoulders. 'I don't think there's any point anymore. I think we're all gonna die in here anyway. I'm just prolonging it, aren't I? I've had enough now.'

I don't answer her; I can't, because she could be right.

'Newbies,' she says.

I look across to the door. Another group of humans has arrived for the cages, and I hear the high-pitched instructions being given by the female Malion. I'm on my knees, staring over the heads of the people in front, and I realise I'm now one of the grubby faces greeting them. And they're looking back with the same scared and bewildered expression that I must have had.

A small boy is looking across at me. He's only about five, with white-blonde hair and big eyes. My heart melts. He's so young and frightened. I don't think I'll ever forget his little face.

Four are thrown into our cage and five, who are already quite big, go straight to green. The others, including the boy, are taken to the cages above.

I hate the way this is starting to feel normal.

A girl stands up, only a few feet away from us. She starts thumping the bars with her fists just as a Malion passes the cage. 'Hey, did you speak to someone?' she yells. 'Did you tell them I'm the daughter of Lord Carlington?'

The Malion ignores her.

'She's off again,' Evie whispers. 'Arrived a day before you did and kept claiming she shouldn't be here and there's been some terrible mistake or something. I'm surprised they haven't punished her more. She did get a rod in the leg, but that's it. She's been quiet for a day or two.'

I look at the girl. She's gripping the bars of the cage and sobbing. I don't want her to get punished again.

I stand up. 'You okay?' I ask.

She turns to me and I see fury behind her fear. 'Do I look okay? I'm not supposed to be here, but no one will listen to me. I've waited and waited, but they're not doing anything.'

'I don't think any of us are supposed to be here,' I say.

'But do you have one of these?' she snaps, pulling at a long chain around her neck. On the end is something I recognise instantly: a red and gold sphere, the same as the soldiers were wearing.

'What is it?' I ask.

'This is why I shouldn't be here, but they're ignoring it and they're not allowed to do that. You wait, there's going to be trouble when my father finds out. I was just visiting a friend, that's all. I should never have been taken. There must be something wrong with their scanners. This should have been detected.'

Her voice is loud. She wants the Malion on the far side

of the room to hear everything. The other prisoners look just as baffled as me.

'Why would wearing that make any difference?' I ask. 'Who gave it to you?'

She suddenly looks uneasy, and the Malion's eyes are now fixed on her. The mood in the cage has shifted, become tense.

'Because I'm not like you,' she says calmly, her voice lowering.

She flicks a strand of blonde hair away from her eyes. Even with a few days of cage grime, she still looks well-groomed. Nobody looks that good these days, not even on Earth. She's older than me, maybe eighteen. Her clothes look expensive, designer, and more suited to a nightclub. People don't dress like that anymore. And her pretty face is unspoiled by the sunken cheeks and grey skin that the rest of us suffer from. She's right, I think, she's not like me.

'You don't know anything, any of you. I still have a life on the surface. A flat, a job, things I need to be doing. This isn't my fate, it's yours. I should've been safe.' She turns back to the bars and hits them again. 'Get your boss out here now. I need to go home.'

She gets her wish, the boss has arrived, but maybe not the one she wanted. Jaxz shoves his hand through the bars, grabs the chain and yanks it from the girl's throat, chucking it to the ground by my foot.

I pick it up to give it back to her, but before I can, Jaxz slams the punishment rod deep into the girl's stomach. The whole thing is glowing red hot as more and more smoke fills the air. The girl shudders, screaming, but all we can do is watch in horror, helpless to do anything. I touch my arm, reminded of the terrible pain. I can't imagine what she must be going through. Younger children cry and bury their faces in their hands. I look on.

She twists, her face contorted. Finally Jaxz stops and she collapses to the floor, smoke rising from her charred body. I cover my nose against the smell of burned flesh.

Two Malions march into the cage, the carpet of prisoners parting to form a narrow pathway for them as they drag the girl's lifeless body away. Her eyes are staring – dead.

Jaxz leaves without a word. Everyone is stunned into silence. I carefully sit down, clutching the girl's pendant in my hand. Gold lines swirl across its red enamel surface.

'He killed her,' I whisper. I shudder as I remember the look of pleasure on Jaxz's face.

'She should've kept her mouth shut,' Evie says.

'But what she was saying . . . '

Evie looks at me. 'Oh come on, you don't think she was serious? She was pulling a scam, trying to get out of here. I guess it worked . . . Or backfired. Whatever.'

'But I've seen these before,' I say, holding the pendant. 'The soldiers on Earth have started wearing them too.'

'Maybe she nicked one.'

'No, something is going on . . . '

I try to think back. The fake-sounding radio reports that never added up; the sudden lack of any kind of military presence when the raids were on. Mum always made up a reason to defend the government but Dad and I knew it didn't make sense. And he lost his job as a government scientist. Did Dad know something more? I have a really bad feeling about this.

'Lola, she was just a crazy. You get them all the time in here, believe me.'

'Maybe,' I say, slipping the pendant into my blazer pocket – but I'm thinking: Or *maybe not.*

After two more claustrophobic and hellish sleeps in the cage I feel weak, too weak for someone who's supposed to be saving the world. Saving the world – now *that's* a joke. I have to eat more because I don't want to die, not before I've found Dad.

'Evie, you're hurting me,' I say.

Evie has fallen asleep and her head is a dead weight on my shin. I try to move my leg from under her, but she just grabs it tighter, groans and nestles her face into my trousers. I can't be bothered to try again. My stomach hurts. It feels hollow, like there's finally nothing left inside.

A trolley with no wheels glides towards the corner of the cage. The prisoners all begin to sit up. I prod Evie.

'What's that?' I ask pointing at the trolley.

She lifts her head, follows my finger and sneers up her nose. 'Snack time, but I don't want anything. We haven't had one of these for a while. If you want something you'll have to catch it – but I really wouldn't bother if I were you.' She puts her head back down and closes her eyes.

'What do you mean, catch it?' I frown. But her words soon become clear when a Malion begins throwing things into the cage from the trolley. They look like small nuggets of bread. Kids and older children dive for the pieces of food, catching them in mid-air with desperate enthusiasm. It's like we're animals in a zoo and it's feeding time. People cry out as they're trodden on and kicked.

I want some, but there is no way I'm ever getting any. The others are way too quick and nimble. Besides, Evie has fallen asleep again. I can't even move, let alone leap into the air.

'Here.'

I turn. Torrin is crouched down by the cage. Shock must be etched all over my face, because he gives me a cautious nod then hands me two pieces of bread through the bars.

'I've read the scans from your bowl. You haven't been eating anything. They'll call you in if you don't eat,' he says. His voice is low, controlled.

'I can't eat something that might be . . .' I can't even say it anymore.

'Then eat the bread.'

I turn one of the nuggets over and over between my fingers. 'If I eat this will it make me want to . . . need to, eat more?' I look directly at him and I can tell that he knows what I mean.

'No, the bread is fine.'

I'm not sure if I believe him. But I do need to eat. I tear a tiny piece from the hard nugget and stare down at it. Then I look at him. His pale skin is almost perfect, apart from a tiny scar above his right eyebrow. His hair hangs over one eye, but the other is as bright as before.

'I didn't think you were speaking to me. I guess I did sound a bit desperate the other day but given my circumstances . . .'

'I came here to give you the bread. That's my job.'

'Okay.' I don't know what else to say.

'Is your arm healing?'

I shrug. 'I don't know.' I can feel the pressure of my tears building, but I don't want to cry in front of him. 'I think the material from my blazer is stuck to it. I can't pull it away because it hurts too much.'

'It will heal.'

'Will it?'

'Yes,' he answers, but for some reason his bluntness causes one rogue tear to escape.

'Get me out of here?' I say, playing my last card. 'Help me find my dad?'

'I can't.'

His answer is clear. I don't think anything I say will change his mind.

Torrin stands, but I'm still pinned down by Evie.

'Eat the bread. That's an order. This will be over soon.' He walks away, and doesn't look back.

Jaxz stares at Torrin as he passes, and then looks to me. I keep my eyes fixed on the floor. What did he mean by 'It will be over soon'? It didn't sound good. I wipe the back of my hand across my face as more tears flow. The trolley has moved away and everyone is beginning to settle back down again. A few muted scuffles occur over the last remaining nuggets, but it's clear no one wants to be punished so they're soon resolved.

My fingers tear at the bread. I try eating it. It's so dry. I'm in real danger of dislocating my jaw by trying to chew it, but at least it's food and not my Musket. It tastes of nothing and scratches the sides of my throat as I force it down. I need some water.

A girl to my right is looking at me. I don't want to stare back, but after a while of feeling her eyes gnawing into me, I glance over. She looks angry. I frown back and shrug, but her expression remains. It isn't until I've woken Evie and freed my leg so I can go and get a drink that she speaks. I'm trying to pick my way through the tangle of bodies and then she's on her feet, behind me.

'Why are you getting special treatment?' she spits. 'Only bin here five minutes. Gonna be his little pet, are we? We got a name for girls like you – wanna hear it?'

I spin round. 'What did you say?'

'You heard me. Why should we have to fight for a piece of bread and you get it handed to yer, like some princess?'

I look around; Jaxz and the Malions don't seem to have spotted us yet.

'I missed breakfast, that's all,' I say calmly.

I look over to Evie for support. She is watching, but then turns away. Can't say I blame her.

'I need to go and get some water. I don't want any trouble.' I try to walk away but the girl grabs my arm. 'Get off me,' I say.

'Or you'll do what? Call your boyfriend?'

Her face is too near mine. I can smell her rank breath and rancid armpits. I want to gag. I kick her in the shin, really hard, just as she takes a fistful of my hair and yanks.

I hear some of it rip from my scalp; the pain so intense that I scream. Another girl is on her feet and a well-placed punch buries itself into my hollow stomach, followed by a foot slamming into my side. I can hear chants of, 'Fight, fight, fight . . .'

I fall to the ground, winded and struggling to get my breath. I need to get up, but the pain is too much and I'm too weak from lack of food. Why isn't anyone helping me? Where's Evie? Another foot bangs into my spine, but my scream seems futile. How can this be happening?

Through the haze of confusion I hear the two girls cry out in pain. I look up to see at least three Malions in the cage. They're beating the girls to the ground with their rods. Powerful blow after powerful blow until the girls collapse into shuddering heaps. But they're still alive – just.

The cage doors swing open and another two Malions come rushing in, trampling on anyone who doesn't move out of their way. A burning rod is thrust into my thigh and I screech, my breath trapped in my throat. The pain is indescribable as I'm dragged across the floor of the cage with the two girls. I try to resist, shout that it wasn't my fault, but they don't seem to be listening and we're flung out of the cage like three discarded rag dolls.

The girls scream like a pair of wild animals as they're taken away. Suddenly I'm being lifted into the air by someone. I clamp my mouth shut, not wanting to express my pain. I look up at my carrier – it's Torrin.

'Take her to the east room.' The words are fierce, and they belong to Jaxz.

'What?' Torrin says.

'You heard me – that's an order.'

'Yes, of course,' Torrin replies.

He carries me effortlessly towards the door. It automatically opens and I'm out. I didn't plan it this way, but somehow I've done it. I've made it out of the cages.

Chapter Eleven

We're back in the grey corridor. We seem to be heading towards one of the four rooms I saw when I first arrived. The door slides open as soon as Torrin waves the back of his ringed hand across it. We go in. The room is dark. A blue light, from a spot on the ceiling, smothers everything in a dull glow, and it's cold in here, like a fridge. The room is empty apart from a small sink in the corner at the back. A shelf is above it and a cupboard below.

'Where are we?' I ask as he places me down on the hard metal floor. The room smells of raw meat, like the butchers shop that used to be on Dawkins Road. I always hated going in there.

'You don't need to know.'

'Am I in big trouble . . . The fight?' I try to stand up, but he gently pushes me back down.

'Yes.'

That one word makes me shiver, his tone as cold as the room itself. I give it one last try.

'Please, help me . . .'

He glares at me. 'I should never have helped you before. You've . . . I've drawn someone's attention to you and that was a big mistake.'

'Do you mean that Malion?' I remember the way he had stared at the two of us. The way he looked at Torrin — and at me.

Torrin turns away from me and goes to the work station in the corner. 'I need to deal with your wounds — that's my job.'

'Fixing me, not feeding me?' I snap.

He looks back over his shoulder, his eyes the brightest thing in the room. But they're wet. Are they tears? But why? He returns, carrying a small tray of bottles and medical implements which clatters as he places it down on the floor. He crouches beside me.

'His name is Jaxz.' I don't tell him I already know his name. I can't risk getting Evie into trouble. 'He's the highest ranking worker on this ship. Now be quiet, or . . .'

I see him give a brief glance upwards and I follow it to another of those holes high up on the wall. He looks worried. Terrified, even.

'What's in there?'

'Nothing,' he says, returning his focus to me, but I can tell there's something he's not telling me.

'What's wrong?'

'Be quiet.' He grabs a small bottle from the tray. Taking my arm, he sprays the clear fluid from the bottle all over the burned area. I force myself to look at my arm. A circular portion of my blazer is dissolving, including the material stuck to the skin. It's cold but it doesn't hurt.

'Are you a doctor?'

'I have medical training that can be used on humans, yes.'

I really want to hate him, but for some reason I don't. He sprays the liquid on to my leg. This stings more – I guess because the burn is fresher. I wince, and as the material dissolves it reveals my blistered wound in all its red-raw glory.

'Please describe how much pain you're in,' he says without expression.

'Quite a bit.'

'Thank you. But I must treat the whole burn, you do understand that?'

I nod.

He puts the bottle back and picks up a large tub of what can only be described as green blancmange, although I'm guessing it isn't.

'You'll need to take off your blazer,' he orders.

I do as he asks, being careful to ensure that the blue pot doesn't fall from the pocket, and trying not to groan too loudly as my ribs protest against the movement. I consider my next question.

'Why are you fixing me up?'

No reply. I try another.

'What's going to happen to me?'

He doesn't answer, but I see his eyes flick involuntarily to the hole near the ceiling. My heart begins to pound. Whatever it is, I don't think I'm going to like it. He rips the material on my trouser leg, and I see the full extent of the burn for the first time. There is a ring of painfully inflamed skin spreading out from the puncture wound.

Torrin picks up a metal spatula and uses it to scoop a large dollop of the green substance on to my skin. He smears it gently over my injuries. It stings again, even though I can tell he's trying to be careful. He massages it into the blistered skin and all traces of the green goo are quickly absorbed. It has a peculiar smell, which lingers in the air.

'The scars will remain, but you should be in less pain.'

'Thanks.'

'Take this.' He hands me a tiny circle of blue paper. 'I wouldn't normally give you this but . . . put it on your tongue. It'll dissolve in a second and help ease the pain even more.'

I look at it, unsure whether to trust him. 'What is it?'

'You're in pain every time you move, that's obvious. This will help . . . help you to cope.'

'Cope with what?'

'Just take it, please,' he says.

If I'm going to get out of here I need at least to be able to walk. I stare down at the almost transparent disc on my fingertip. It could be anything. One half of me is screaming, *it will kill you,* the other half telling me I have no choice. I take the gamble and place it on my tongue.

Torrin stays still, watching me. It fizzes a little at first, and then across my taste buds spills a strange flavour – it's like lemon mixed with pepper, but it's not unpleasant.

After a few seconds my ribs feel easier when I breathe; maybe the gamble has paid off. I'm not dead – at least not yet.

With the dull ache gone from my limbs, I feel stronger. Torrin takes a scanner from the tray and presses it to my temple. The familiar hum interrupts the silence of the room.

'Am I healthy?' I say.

'Better than you were.'

He gets up and walks across the room to wash his hands in the basin by the work station. 'You will stay in here now,' he says with his back to me.

'Why?'

'Because humans who cause trouble are never allowed back in the cages,' he says. 'The door will be locked.'

I'm a prisoner again, and that's not what I want.

'I'm assuming you're not going to try and escape?' he asks, as though reading my thoughts. I suddenly wonder if he can.

'Not unless you think I'd stand a good chance,' I reply.

'No.'

'That good?' I say. But he doesn't know how determined I can be.

He walks towards the doorway then stops, his hand resting on the top of his head, as if frozen to his thoughts. I know, without a doubt, this has to be my best chance.

I don't have time to think. I take my blazer and slip it

back on. I don't really want to wear it anymore, it's rancid, but the pockets are deep. I stand up, the butchers' smell of the room and my own fear clogging into a lump at the back of my throat.

'Why did you treat my burns? Tell me what's going to happen to me in this room after you leave.'

He spins back round. There is a look in his eyes that I can't fathom at first, and then I do . . . It's guilt.

'You really want to know?'

I nod.

'No . . . I can't.'

'Please.'

He takes a breath. 'I fixed you because the Arlatans don't like to eat burned flesh.'

We stare at each other. Suddenly I can't breathe. 'What . . .'

'You haven't guessed?' he says. His eyes are flickering like flames again. 'You're just food to the Arlatans. That's your fate – as simple and as uncomplicated as that.'

'F-food? What do you mean . . . they *eat us*?' I know I must have got that wrong, because it sounds all wrong when it comes out of my mouth.

But Torrin's expression doesn't change.

He paces to the other side of the room. 'I shouldn't have told you. You shouldn't know any of this before . . .' He shakes his head.

'Please, I want to know. I need to.'

I'm trembling, but try to hide it from him. He won't say another word if he knows I'm getting upset. I'd considered many horrible things, apart from my optimistic new-life-in-paradise theory. Slavery had always been the worst idea I'd had, but this? This is horrific.

'They keep some of us alive. The scan you had in the processing unit when you first arrived, it shows if you have any skills that the Arlatans could find useful. If you do then you are made to work for them. That's what happened to me.'

'And if you don't?' I swallow hard. I'm guessing that this answer will apply to me.

'The processing unit also weighs you. If you're over a certain weight, which most adults are, then you go straight to . . .' He turns away from me. I hear him take in another huge gulp of air – he's struggling. 'If you're underweight, like kids, then you go to the cages to grow and be fattened up. The very old are usually . . . discarded. Their flesh isn't tender enough.'

It's as if he's talking about animals. I think of the obese greens. This is nothing more than a farm and a slaughter-house. Patrick and Aimee – they're all right for now. But my dad . . . I have to know more.

'The food, what do they put in the food they give us?'

'It's a chemical that makes you eat more so you'll grow faster, meatier. They want you totally dependant on meal times so you'll worry less about . . . about what's going to happen to you.'

I wrap my arms around myself. This is insane. 'The adults, where do the adults go? You didn't say where they went.'

My dad's face is in my head, it won't leave. My amazing dad, smiling at me from my memories, so real, just like I

remember him. I wrap my fingers around the blue pot —
my need for it is looking more and more likely.

'You don't need to know anymore,' he says.

'My dad, Torrin . . . I have to know,' I cry.

He gnaws at the inside of his cheek. 'The humans that
meet the correct weight go to cold storage — a facility at
the bottom of each Prisoner Ship. There the prisoners are
frozen, to be used and shipped when necessary.'

His words are entering my brain, swirling around, but
not sinking in. He isn't saying this to me. I have to be
dreaming.

'Take me there, to my dad.'

Torrin looks at me, and for a second I see pity in his
eyes, but then the rigid mask is back. 'He'll be dead.'

'No, don't say that. I have to see him, I need proof,
Torrin. I won't . . . I c-can't believe what you're telling me
unless I see it for myself.' Now I'm begging, pleading
with him to do this one last thing for me.

'No. And they'd kill me too if I helped you.'

I bury my face in my hands. Of course he won't help
me. Why should he? I'm just one prisoner out of
hundreds.

'I'm sorry if I gave you false hope,' he says, 'but this is
how it is now, the only way.'

This isn't the only way, I think.

'You should sit back down again. The blue disc I gave
you, it was more than just a painkiller. Soon it will knock
you out, and help you . . .'

'Help me to cope . . .' I finish. 'Yes, I remember.'

He doesn't say anymore. He sweeps his hand and ring

across a small lighted panel on the door and it opens.

I know I have to act now, while I'm still able to. If he's not going to help me find Dad, then I'll find him myself. The small metal tray is still lying beside me on the floor. I try not to think of Torrin as the boy who tried to save me from the Leeches, but as what he really is — my enemy, a prison guard — because it's the only way I'll be able to do this.

His back is to me. I pick up the tray and the contents fall nosily to the floor. Torrin turns, his mouth gaping. In one forceful swipe I smash the metal tray into his head with every ounce of energy I have left.

Chapter Twelve

He lies on the floor, absolutely still.

I resist the urge to bend down and check him. Instead I throw the tray away, yank the ring from his finger, and sprint over his body and out of the doorway. The clattering of the discarded tray still rings in my ears as I run as fast as I can down the corridor. I hold my side as a stabbing pain grips and twists at my muscles – but at least I'm moving. I can't have killed him, he can't be dead. Should I have left the door open?

I have no idea what I'm doing – why do I never have a plan? I turn left at the end of the corridor. I don't think I'm going the same way I came in. There's a break in the wall up ahead, a recess. I slow down as I get nearer, moving in closer to the side. I'm exhausted, running just those few steps has almost wiped me out. I'm still so weak from lack of food, or is it the painkiller?

As I reach the recess, I scc a large glass panel stretching at least six metres wide along the back of it. It's dark inside, like a viewing room. Tentatively I walk over to the window, throwing a last-minute glance over my shoulder. I look down through the window.

A brightly lit area is spread out below. I hold my breath, fearing that my nervous gasps are likely to get me heard and killed at any second. But I don't understand what I'm seeing.

There are babies, hundreds and hundreds of babies all encased in clear circular cribs moving around the room on a network of cogs, like giant Ferris wheels. Malions and some humans are tending to them. It's calm and serene, just like a giant nursery.

My heart dips as I realise what this is. These human babies must be the new stock. This really is a farm and we're the animals. I bite down so hard on my thumbnail I'm in danger of cracking a tooth.

One of the Malions is staring up at the window. Can she see me? Why else would she be looking? I slowly back away. I need to hide, but pain shoots through my side like an arrow piecing my gut – so much for Torrin's painkiller. But I wonder how long I've got before it really takes effect and I'm knocked out?

Why did I take it? Why did I trust him? My bruised body is warning me to rest. I stumble back against the wall. But as I put my hand to the surface to save myself, it touches something horrible, something wet – slime. All the walls are coated in slime.

I lift my hand to look. It's covered in a thick layer of the stuff. I wipe my hand down my trouser leg.

Then I run.

Is it the same slime from my nightmares? If I look up, will a monster be there? No, there's nothing – nothing above me, I'm sure of it. I'd be dead by now if there was. It's not real. I hobble along the corridor. There's nowhere to hide. I stagger on, limping and praying I don't see anyone. My legs are getting weaker.

I desperately need to stop; the pain is intolerable, like a severe cramp. I can't see properly, everything is fuzzy. There are two doors at the end of the corridor. I push one but it doesn't budge. There's an illuminated panel between the doors and I wave Torrin's ring across it. One of the doors slides open. I sigh with relief. A room. Somewhere to hide.

Once inside I close the door with another sweep of the ring. I push it over my thumb, because it's too big for any of my fingers. The room is dim. It's empty, or so I think at first. Then I see the two bodies lying on the floor, an amber light shining down on each one from above.

I cover my mouth to stop myself from screaming – and from being sick. I blink, trying to clear the fog from my vision. The two bare bodies are facing the ceiling, vacant of breath or soul, but I recognise them. The two girls from the cages. Is it my fault they're dead? If I hadn't taken the bread from Torrin, the girl wouldn't have goaded me. The girl whose kick is causing me so much pain now looks so young, the anger I witnessed gone from her pale face. Why did they have to kill them?

I move away, back into the corner and slide down the wall. I cradle my legs to my chest and cry, harder than I've ever cried. This place is nothing but a living hell.

I hope Patrick is in a cage somewhere, it seems the safest place for him to be. But then Dad creeps into my head. I've tried really hard not to think about him too much. He's an ex-rugby player, a hefty weight. I know he won't be in any of the cages. But maybe they've kept him alive, like they had Torrin. He's a scientist; surely that would be useful to them? I already know Musket's gone – I've had to accept that.

I can't think anymore. My head hurts. I almost wish I was incapable of caring. Maybe it would be easier if they were all dead, then I'd only have one thing on my mind – killing as many Arlatans as I could.

Suddenly I think of something else. I look up. In the wall, near the ceiling, is one of the holes. Are they tunnel openings? Now I realise: this room is identical to the one I was just in – the work station in the corner, the tunnel, the cold air, even the gut-wrenching smell of raw meat and . . . and that peculiar odour of the green goo. The girls must have been treated too. In fact, the only difference in this room is the colour of the light shining from above.

'What is this place?' I whisper to myself. But then I hear something, a scraping sound from above my head. I freeze, holding my breath.

There is movement in the mouth of the tunnel. The sound of rasping . . . something breathing and squelching. As the source of the sound emerges into the amber light,

I have to force back a scream.

It's my nightmare. Here and now, in this room.

A great mound of thick, black-scaled flesh, like a giant slug, with slime dripping from every enormous pore. A grotesque, diamond-shaped jaw. Rows of razor-like teeth. A series of lumps across the top of its head like stumpy antennae. And three large red eyes – illuminated, cold and alert.

And then it opens its mouth wide and its head shoots down to the floor, the neck extending. A loud squeal of excitement fills my ears, then the creature grabs one of the girls between those jaws and squeezes down, shaking the body from side to side. Blood splatters the walls and there's a sickening crack of bones. Groans of satisfaction gurgle from the monster's throat then, in one backwards flick of its bulbous head, it swallows the body whole.

I want to throw up, right here, right now. Was this my fate, too? What Torrin was preparing me for? How could he?

My breath catches in my throat and it's enough to make the Arlatan stop. Its head turns towards me. Every muscle I have tightens. I don't move a single millimetre. His reptilian eyes are wide, searching the room for the cause of the sound.

Don't see me, please don't see me, I pray. *I'm dead. I'm so dead.*

A second feels like an hour. But my corner is dark. I'm hidden from its sight. Maybe the three red eyes can't see like human eyes. But can it smell me? It's moving across the ceiling, slithering closer and closer. It's above me. I don't move. Its head stretches down towards me and I can feel its breath on my hair. It reeks of the sickly stench. I'm shaking, and jump as a loud growl erupts from the monster's throat. I clasp my hands to my head and the ring on my thumb vibrates slightly.

Don't eat me.

To my relief and shock, it slowly moves away. The lure of the remaining body is clearly too tempting and the Arlatan makes quick work of devouring it, as brutally and noisily as the first. Then it leaves just as it came, except now, blood is dripping from its mouth, human blood. It curls itself back into the tunnel seemingly unfazed to having had an audience. I look down at the ring on my thumb. Did I imagine it vibrating? Maybe it gives off a signal or something. Because surely the Arlatan knew I was here. It must have thought I was a worker – protected.

But those poor girls.

I sit huddled in my corner for a few minutes, rocking away my terror, making sure the creature has gone. The amber light changes to blue, like the one in the room I was in before. An amber light clearly means dinner-time. I want to be sick again, and I try – not that there's anything to bring up. I have to get out of here and find Dad, I just *have* to. Then we can make a plan, because he can't be dead. I need him.

I struggle to my feet and swipe the ring against the panel to leave the room. I'm desperate to get away from the blood-soaked walls and the smell. My head is swimming and I feel so tired, but I'm not going to give in to whatever Torrin gave me. I must keep going. I hurry back towards the recess that looks over the nursery, and shoot inside just as a line of about twenty prisoners march by, led by a tall, spindly Malion.

They're all greens. It was hard to see in the darkness of the cages, but now I can. They really are obese. Shuffling along in one long line. Plump and ready for consumption. I can see the tattooed bands on their wrists, like the blue one around mine. Some have more than one band, a stack of different colours. I guess they get a band for each cage they've been in. I know Evie has two. I notice they now have a black band above the green. The one they were given as they left. Does that mean they've reached their full-weight?

I watch from the shadows as they pass by. I want to reach out, but I don't. Most are staring down at their feet, their hands bound together with gold ropes. They are quiet, subdued, drugged. One girl, with a long ginger braid down her back, spots me, but there is nothing in her eyes. Whoever she once was, that person no longer exists. They don't know where they're going, or what's going to happen to them. Maybe that's best.

Where *are* they going? And then it hits me.

Cold storage – exactly where I need to be.

Chapter Thirteen

I follow the line of greens at a safe distance, staying close to the wall, my heart racing so fast I feel faint against its force.

Each passageway looks the same, a labyrinth of grey. I look up at each tunnel opening as I pass, praying not to see any red eyes staring back at me.

Another Malion is at the rear of the column of greens, hitting and shoving them forwards if they dare to dawdle. They stop and I drop back a little. Beside them, on the surface of an otherwise blank wall, is a large shimmering square – white with flecks of red swirling deep inside it. Some kind of force field? It's bigger than any normal doorway.

'Stand apart once inside,' says the Malion, 'and do not

touch each other.' She waves her hand across the face of the square.

What is it? A lift? It has to be – Torrin said cold storage was at the bottom of the Prisoner Ship. I hate lifts. But this isn't the time for my stupid claustrophobia to act up.

I watch as one by one they walk through the force field and disappear inside. Once the last Malion is in, I run over. I make the decision to wait a few minutes, give them time to get out. But what if I lose them?

Impatience wins and I wave the ring across the lift. I step through the force field, my breath whipping away from me as if I've just walked through an icy shower.

I'm inside a box of blinding light, pulsing all around me. I close my eyes to it. Keep calm, I tell myself. But what do I do now? I speak the words. 'Cold storage.' I don't hear my voice and nothing seems to happen.

I take a deep breath, but there's no air – I'm suffocating. Or am I hyperventilating? Should have brought my paper bag with me. The thought makes me feel hysterical. I try to concentrate, keeping as still as I can. I think the words, over and over in my head. *Cold storage. Cold storage . . .*

A weird feeling begins to engulf my entire body. Not painful, just like something crawling beneath my skin, penetrating deep into every organ. I let out a scream, but I don't hear it.

It only lasts a few bizarre seconds and then one side of the box dims, allowing me to see the other side. I step through it and sigh with joy for still being in one piece – alive. I don't think I want to know what just happened to me.

I'm in a large cold room, surrounded by rails of equipment and clothing. I hide behind one of them. Along every wall, hanging from big black hooks, are silver coats. And everything – from floor to ceiling – is covered in a layer of fine white ice crystals.

The place is deserted, apart from the group of greens over on the far side. I see both Malions putting on one of the coats. The greens don't get offered one; I guess they won't need to keep warm. I desperately want to help them, but I can't think of a way. I'm so, so cold my brain hurts.

I spot a glass kiosk, raised about halfway up the back wall. I count at least four figures inside. One Malion and three humans, or maybe they're like Torrin. Workers, I guess. I step back a little further behind the rail, trying not to dislodge the tubes and bottles hanging from it. I wish Patrick was here. He'd know what to do, he knows everything. I never thought I'd miss him so much, but right now I'd do anything to be listening to one of his awful jokes. Where is he? What if he's too big for the cages? He's taller than me, but he is skinny. Don't let him be here. Don't let Dad be here.

I grab a coat, slip my arms into it and lift the hood. It's a heavy silver material with a thick rubbery lining, and it drowns me – the weight of it dragging on my puny shoulders. But I do feel warmer.

My nerves are almost shot now, the dread of finding Dad threatening to push me over the edge. *Don't think about what this place is, you can cope*, I keep telling myself, over and over again. And he may not even be here. He may be alive as a worker, swearing because he's left the pills at home, and hoping I'm on my way to help – hoping I've given the folder to the authorities. Huh, some hope. How could I have messed everything up so badly?

There's a creepy silence here, like the whole ship is dead. The greens disappear into another lift, but I don't follow. I have a feeling I don't want to be going where they're going. A door on the opposite side of the room catches my eye. I walk towards it, my insides twisting like a rollercoaster. I try to keep out of sight of the workers in the kiosk by staying close to the rails. But when I do glance up my heart almost stops.

It's Patrick. I can't believe it. He's talking to another human, his animated hand gestures confirming it's him. He's alive. My wish has been answered! I reach the door, holding my chest as the feeling of relief overwhelms me. I think I'm going to pass out. Is this shock or has that stupid painkiller won its battle to subdue me?

I straighten up. I want to shout out to Patrick, but I know I can't – there are too many workers around him. But he's safe, for now, that's the main thing. And I still have a job to do.

I face the door. My gut is telling me that what I need is behind it. I pull my coat tighter around my body. My nose is like a frozen piece of putty stuck to my face and my toes went numb ages ago.

I take a large gulp of the cold air, the back of my throat prickling with the sudden icy intake. I've never felt so alone. The metal door is like a freezer door in a restaurant. I can see a skin of sparkling ice all over it – just looking at it makes me shiver and want to leave. But I won't – I can't.

Whatever this is, I have to go in.

I wave Torrin's ring across the illuminated panel on the door and it silently slides downwards. As I walk in, my legs begin to buckle beneath my body.

My eyes aren't capable of opening any wider as I stare ahead. I can't quite absorb the horror spread out in front of me. My stomach clenches and I crumple all the way to the icy ground.

There are hundreds, no, *thousands* of bodies frozen in blocks of solid ice, like marble statues. Standing upright in their frozen coffins.

My warm breath swirls like smoke from my mouth as I struggle to remind my body to breathe, and my hand slips on the ice as I try to push myself up. Managing to get to my feet, I stagger to the wall behind me. But someone is approaching. I stiffen, ready to run. He stops a few metres away, encased in a similar coat to mine. He has gloves and boots on; maybe I should have hunted around for some of those too. He puts a hand up and nods, as if greeting me. I do the same in response.

What if it's Patrick? But I can't be sure, and he wouldn't have had time to get from the kiosk to here. Then he takes what looks like a white tea tray from a rack and drops it to the ground, where it hovers like a skateboard with no wheels. He steps on to it and glides effortlessly upwards. He's holding a small device in his hand, which he uses to scan each body as he passes. And then he's out of sight, and I'm alone again.

I guess in this coat I look like any other worker; the

hood practically covers my face. Unless someone gets very close, I think I might be safe. I try to stay upright as I make my way over to the rack, but my legs are trembling, as if they know more than I do about what's coming. It's so achingly cold, like being in a giant deep-freeze. I guess that's exactly what it is.

I tug at one of the tray thingies, but it doesn't leave the rack. I try again, frustrated, but it's stuck fast. I notice one of the lighted panels at the end of the rack and I wave my ring over it. The tray detaches. I thank all my stars I had the sense to take Torrin's ring. A horrible feeling of guilt sweeps over me, as I remember seeing him on the floor of the room, out cold.

But he's the enemy, I tell myself. *He left me to be eaten.*

I drop the tray to the floor and it hovers, just as it had for the worker. I step on and immediately fall off, darting a look in every direction, but no one's here. My legs are so numb it's hard to control them. And I feel so tired, my eyes struggling to stay open. I try again, but my constant shaking is not helping my balance. Four illuminated buttons sit at the end of the tray. I press the left one with my foot and I begin to glide forwards. Gradually I work out the simple method of controlling it and manage to glide to the base of one of the rows.

I don't even know where to start looking. If he's here, then maybe he'll be near the front. He'll have only been here a few days.

I glide past row upon row of bodies, all standing upright, all staring – all dead. I can't see the end of the room, and when I look up I can't see the ceiling either, just more rows of humans stretching up into darkness.

Large metal frames covered in icicles hold the frozen coffins in place. Small piercing white lights illuminate each of the rows, casting spooky shadows across the corpses. A mixture of cold greys, whites and the palest blues surround me. The whole thing resembles a horror movie, but I don't fear these dead bodies suddenly coming back to life. In fact, I want them to – all of them.

Some of the frames have labels attached. But I don't understand any of the strange symbols. Maybe it's where they're going to be shipped. Maybe if they have a label they're the latest to arrive – like a use-by date. I see one with symbols in bright red ink. I head to the end of the row and stop.

It's worth a try and I have nothing else to go on. I look down; I'm about three rows up from the icy floor. I hold on to the frame beside me, feeling off balance again. It wouldn't be a good idea to give in to the painkiller up here.

I look straight ahead, but I have a bad feeling and I don't know why. I let go of the frame seconds before my skin has a chance to stick to the freezing metal. I glide slowly away.

I try to swallow the knot blocking the back of my throat, but it won't budge. I look up at each face as I pass – women, men, all shapes and sizes, all nameless to me. But someone, somewhere will be missing them. I think of people I know that have been taken: my beautiful Aunty Helen, always smiling; Ricky my lifeguard cousin. Are they here? Are they dead?

I must have passed at least sixty on this row, maybe more, and with every one I'm beginning to feel hopeful. Maybe Dad isn't here. He's a scientist – useful. He's still alive.

But then everything apart from my pounding heart begins to slow. And my whole world starts to crumble.

'Dad,' I choke.

It's him. I stop the glider and stare at the white face behind the veil of clear ice. His pale blue eyes are wide open. I can see the little rugby scar on his chin and the eagle tattoo on the top of his arm, which he got on a trip to Thailand in his twenties. And now there's something else: a black band of colour around his wrist, the colour of a full weight. Like the greens were given. Our quality mark – our branding. It makes me sick.

He'll never call me squirrel again, the nickname he gave me because I'd hide food in my bedroom when I was little. He'll never tell me off for playing my music too loud, or give me advice that always made perfect sense. Dad always listened, always had faith in me, but now . . .

I hold my stomach as the reality of finding him floods me, and the tears, which I've tried really hard to hold on to, burst out.

'What do I do now, Dad? I thought you'd be alive, that you'd have a plan.' I crouch down, holding on to the sides of the platform, and sob out the excruciating pain.

This is all my fault. I know it is. I caused this to happen. I've messed everything up, as always. *You should have been home, Lola.* My mum was right.

I look up at him, my vision blurred through a film

124

of tears, desperate for him to hear me, to hear my confession.

'I shouldn't have bunked off, Dad. I'm so sorry I let you down. I wanted to help you, but Mum stopped me. And I blamed her. But it was all my fault, she was just trying to protect me – I know that now.' I wrap one arm around my chest, trying to ease the ache. 'I want to make it up you, to make you proud, put this right. But what if . . .'

I close my eyes. 'What if I can't do it?' is what I want to say. I ruined a lot more than just our family that day. I ruined Dad's plan to fight back. He shouldn't have been taken. It wasn't his time, he wasn't prepared. And he cried out to me . . . He needed my help. I think of the blue folder still lying on his desk that no one on Earth knows about. I've failed him. I'm no better prepared than he was, and I had the advantage of time. I should have got the folder to someone. I should have waited.

I force a hand across my tear-coated face and try to pull myself together before someone hears me. I have to get out of here. Staying crouched, I lower myself to the ground.

'I love you, Dad.' I whisper, blowing a kiss towards his icy form as I sink further away, trying not to think of what will eventually happen to him. That thought is way too horrific and painful.

I'm so weak by the time I reach the floor, I can hardly move. For some reason I can't get the platform to work anymore, it's not responding, so I leave it where it is. My hands and feet are hurting, like pins are being jammed through my skin.

As I try to get my bearings, it's soon apparent that I've moved a long way from where I came in. Where was the door? I walk, shuffle and slip, struggling to put one foot in front of the other. My head feels light. If someone spots me now, I'm done for. But I don't think I can fight Torrin's painkiller anymore.

As I reach the side of the room my legs give way and I collapse. I fall hard, yelling out, my ribs still pounding from their earlier punishment. I can't get up. Panic wells inside me. If I don't get out I'll freeze in here. But I'm too cold, too numb and too weak.

I try to force myself up, grabbing on to a thin ledge running the length of the wall, but my fingers won't work properly and I tumble back to the ice beneath. The sharp metal rim cuts my fingertips and blood pours out. I can't even feel the pain. My shivering is out of control. I think I'm in shock or something. It's the painkiller – it must be. The room is getting fainter and fainter. I've stayed in this giant tomb for too long, I should have got out sooner.

I shut my eyes. All I want to do is sleep.

I'm sorry, Dad, it's over. I've failed.

Chapter Fourteen

'm playing with Musket on the common, throwing his favourite ball for him to race after. The afternoon sun is hot on my face and the freshly cut grass a lush green. I can see Mum and Dad. They're sitting on the daisy-littered ground, glasses of sparkling wine in their hands. Mum is smiling. I'd forgotten how beautiful she looks when she smiles.

Patrick is trying to read his giant brick of a book on science and technology that my dad gave him for his birthday, but I won't let him. We're laughing like we used to, when our biggest problem was getting Mr Cartwright for double maths and not handing in our homework on time. Musket and I are mucking about, rolling on the grass. I feel so happy.

But it's weird . . . Torrin is here, staring at us from the trees. He's holding a red shoe with a broken buckle. Claudia-Rose, aged five. *How did you creep into my world? Get out.* And something else is wrong – the sun is going in. I don't want to leave the common. Why do I have to leave? It's Torrin's fault . . .

'Lola . . . Lola . . . Wake up . . .'

The voice is in my head, pulling me away from the warmth of my family, my friends – the happiness of my made-up world. But I'm clinging on to it with every ounce of resistance I have.

'Lola!'

I feel warmth on my cheeks and I slowly force open my eyes. My eyelashes are stuck, my tears freezing them together – a reminder of the horror I've just seen. Torrin is leaning over me, his hands cupping my face. His eyes are closed, as if he's concentrating on something. Heat is seeping into my frozen face.

I try to pull away. 'W-what are you doing?' I say, through chattering teeth. 'G-get off me.'

'Don't move,' he whispers.

He's using weird alien powers on me, killing me – murdering me. But I can't move – and more heat floods through my body. He's saving me? Again?

Ignoring my groans of pain, he pulls me to my feet and drags me away. I don't know how far we go but suddenly we're out, back in the room with the equipment and coats and where it's slightly warmer. We stay close to the side, out of sight of the workers in the kiosk – and of Patrick.

'Leave me alone,' I whisper, trying to break away from

his grip.

'Be quiet,' he orders, wrapping his arms around me and closing his eyes again. 'You must get warm or you'll die.'

I struggle, but I'm too weak to make any impression. Torrin is like a furnace, and my whole body is tingling as it begins to thaw. Gradually the feeling returns to my legs, my arms, although my feet remain icy cold.

'What . . . are . . . you?' I say, pushing as hard as I can and finally managing to tear away from him.

He opens his eyes. 'I can control the temperature of my skin. Don't ask me how or why, I just can. I have some human traits – and other non-human ones.'

'You're nothing like a human . . . Nothing like me,' I say.

'No, I'm not,' he says. 'I'm not as stupid.'

'Leave me alone – you shouldn't even be here.'

'Neither should you,' he snaps. 'Your stupidity will get us both killed. If I had alerted anyone to your escape, then we'd both now be locked in one of those rooms.'

'I didn't ask you to come here, though.'

'Well, if I hadn't you'd be dead.'

His words are harsh, but he's right. 'Thank you,' I say, the words sticking in my throat. Although I'm thinking I'd rather die by freezing to death than face what he had had in store for me – being eaten by those monsters.

'I don't want your thanks,' he says. 'Just confirmation that you're feeling warmer.'

'Yes,' I say. I take a deep breath. 'I found him. He's dead – my dad.'

'I know.'

'Of course you do.' Torrin probably brought him here, prepared him for the Arlatans' dinner, like he prepared me.

'You can hate me – knocking me unconscious was proof of that – and I am sorry you had to see your father the way he is. But now we need to leave this place – it is too dangerous to stay.'

I don't know whether I buy his sympathy. But a part of me is strangely relieved that he's alive – that he's here.

The place is still deserted when we get back to the lift. I can't help thinking of the greens and what happened to them. The girl with the beautiful ginger braid. She's probably already dead – a ready meal for the monsters. I look up at the kiosk. It's empty.

'I think I saw my friend, Patrick,' I say. 'I have to speak to him.'

'You can't. If it was him, then be thankful he's alive. He's a worker and not in the cages.'

I suppose he's right. At least I know where he is. Now I just need to work out what to do next.

'Take your coat off. An alarm will sound if it's removed from this area . . . Oh, and I'll have my ring back too, if you don't mind.'

Reluctantly I hand back the black-and-silver ring, unable to think of a way to keep it.

'Fine,' I say.

'Fortunate for you that I had another.'

I shrug, trying not to seem bothered. My own life

doesn't have value anymore, not now Dad is dead. The cold hits my aching body as I take off the coat, but I can't afford to give into it, not again. I hang the coat up, but don't have to endure the cold for long, because Torrin shoves me through the force field and into the lift.

We transport back, the experience no more pleasant second time round. When we step out, Torrin seems distant, nervous. We're in a part of the ship that I don't recognise.

'In here,' he says, opening a door to a room opposite the lift.

He pushes me into what looks like a waiting area. Circles of metal chairs fill the room, each with a white table in the centre. Through a large window at the back I can see Earth – home.

But Torrin is standing between me and the view. I think of the bare room he left me in, how he patched me up only in order to be killed.

'I saw them, you know. The two girls. I saw what happened to them . . . Are you taking me back, so you don't get into trouble? Is that why you came for me?'

'They'll find out you've gone soon enough. And if they catch you, you'll be offered as a snack to the two Arlatans that live on this Prisoner Ship. You're lucky I found you.'

His words disgust me, make me more determined than ever to survive. 'Lucky? I don't think so. I need to find my friends and get them out of here.'

I don't mention that I'm then going to kill him and all his monster friends.

'It's impossible.'

I ignore him and try for the door, but he's quicker and blocks me, his hand locking around my wrist. It hurts.

I try a different tack. 'Please, Torrin, I have to get away from here. You helped me twice, saved my life — what's changed?'

His brow sets into deep furrows. 'You can't help your friends. It's too late. Stop trying or you'll die.'

I try to force my arm from his grip, but I can't. 'My friend, Patrick, the one I told you I saw, the one I came in here with. He's clever, a whiz with computers and stuff. Is that why he was chosen to be kept alive as a worker?'

He looks taken aback by my determination. 'Did you hear me? It's too late!'

'Loud and clear, but I have to know what's happening here. I have to get him out of this place. It's my fault he's here. He was trying to stop me from getting taken by the Leech.'

He sighs and releases my arm. 'It's possible that's the reason he's still alive. The Arlatans don't need anyone to teach them about computers because they're way more advanced than any human. But they use people with the right sort of brain to fix them.'

'Can't they do that themselves?' I frown.

'Not really. Their lifestyle means they've become fat and lazy and they use their limbs less and less. So they gather species like us and the Malions to do their work for them.'

'I didn't even know they had limbs.' I think of their jaws extending to devour those girls.

'They have arms, but they're hidden within their flesh,'

he says. 'They're not dextrous.'

'What did you mean — if Patrick has the right sort of brain?'

Torrin looks at me, his expression softer. 'Don't you think it's strange that everyone on this ship speaks English so well?'

'I don't know. I guess.'

'I can speak three hundred and two languages.'

'So, you're an alien with super-powers — it's hardly surprising,' I say, although there's a part of me that can hardly believe I just said that. Patrick would be laughing, if he was here.

'The languages are injected into a small device which we have implanted in our brain.' He smiles at my screwed-up face. 'The Arlatans studied your planet for a quite some time before attacking it.'

He makes it all sound so normal. 'Did it hurt, being injected?'

'Not really. A couple of hours later you can speak any language fluently. And because my species and the Malions are similar to humans, then they think we can put the human prisoners at ease. I mean, if anyone saw an Arlatan, they'd never stop screaming.'

I think about the device in his head for a moment. 'So you could know everything?'

'Yes, but that's not always such a good idea,' he says. 'Information overload can be painful. That's why your brain has to be compatible. For example, someone non-mathematical would struggle with an injection of complex number programming. Anyway, the Kal don't even use it . . . They're the guards that roll along,' he adds. 'They have weird voice boxes and can't use anything except clicks. But they're not very social creatures anyway. Brute force is their favourite form of communication.'

My hand instinctively goes to the bump under my fringe where the ballam hit me. 'I'm guessing that most of the prisoners never get to know this stuff.'

'No, and I shouldn't be telling you.'

'So, now you have to kill me?'

'I don't want to hurt you, believe me. But . . .' he sighs, 'I'll try to get you somewhere safe.'

'What about my friends? Could you get us back to Earth?'

He shakes his head. 'No, I can't do that – it would be too dangerous.'

As if staying here isn't.

'But if you could . . .'

My hand goes to the blue pot in my pocket. If I got home I could take Dad's folder to someone in charge on Earth and give them the pills. Then trained people could do this properly, not me. Surely Dad would still be proud, if I saved Patrick and Aimee? That I'm thinking of the bigger picture? I mean, what damage could I really do on my own?

But am I a failure for thinking that? A failure for wanting to go home?

But Torrin doesn't answer me, and I feel guilty for asking him. Then I wonder why I feel guilty. He's working for them, practically is one of them. Or is he? I look at him, trying not to see the worker feeding his captives in their cage, but a boy who is as much a victim as I am.

Torrin's fiery eyes are serious. 'Time to go, Lola.'

I don't push him any further; I can't risk alienating him. My dad is dead, and I have no idea how to carry out his plan, or even if that's what he'd expect me to do. But if there's a way to get Patrick and Aimee, and even Evie out of this hell, I have to try.

And if that means using Torrin, then so be it.

'Okay,' I say. 'I'm with you.'

Chapter Fifteen

B ack in the corridor the familiar stench of the cages hangs in the air like an unwanted guest. The smell of unwashed flesh seems to seep through the walls, strangling my senses. At least I'm not going back to that.

We start walking. I'm not sure where Torrin is taking me, but we've not gone far when I hear loud footsteps coming towards us.

'Shh . . .' Torrin whispers, pulling both my hands behind my back.

My heart sinks as a large Malion appears from around the corner. It's him. His skin is a deeper red than the females, and his dark blue hair is cropped short and spiked up at crazy angles. It's Jaxz.

'Don't say a word,' Torrin whispers as he grips my arm.

The Malion glares at us. 'What are you doing in this part of the ship?'

'She got away from me,' Torrin laughs. It sounds forced. 'I was bringing her back to you. She can certainly run.'

I shoot Torrin a look of confusion, but he doesn't return it. What is he doing?

'Lively little thing, is she?' Jaxz grins, showing a row of pale pointed teeth. 'Thought she might be. And very pretty for a human, don't you think?' He reaches out and touches my face. His long blue nails scrape across my cheek. 'Caught my eye as soon as she arrived.'

Torrin tightens his grip on my arm. His expression is suddenly rigid. 'She's okay, I suppose.'

'Oh, she's more than okay. Some humans have such dark eyes – yes, she's very pretty. A perfect candidate for Room Zero. As we discussed . . .'

Torrin merely nods.

My mind is buzzing. What is Room Zero? And what have they discussed?

'Good. The Arlatans will have such fun with this one on a live feast night.' He laughs, but it's a cold, inhuman sound. 'They like the lively ones.'

'If you say so,' Torrin replies, his tone unreadable.

The Malion holds out his hand. 'I'll take her now. We need to replace those that were ripped last week.'

Replace those that were ripped. I can guess what that means. I want to run. I've never wanted to run so much in my entire life. But how far would I get? Keep calm and wait for the right moment, I tell myself. But it's the hardest thing I've ever done.

Torrin hesitates and Jaxz gives a low snarl, like an animal. 'Give her to me.'

Torrin flashes me a look. His eyes are turning a dark amber colour, darker than I've ever seen them, and his grip goes from warm to burning in a matter of seconds. Then just as suddenly, to ice.

He pushes me to Jaxz. 'Take her, then.'

So much for taking me to a safe place. It was all just a scam to get me to go with him. He was always going to hand me over, to betray me. And to think I almost trusted him. I should have got away when I had the chance.

'Let's go.' Jaxz grasps the top of my arm, making me wince.

'I can walk,' I say. 'You don't have to drag me.'

'Feisty too? That'll be popular. I do love humans – they're so endearing. Very tasty, too.'

'Get lost,' I snap.

Jaxz laughs again. 'You humans are splendid, you really are.' But he removes his hand from my arm. He isn't holding me.

Torrin looks terrible, the light in his eyes almost extinguished. I was a fool to think he'd ever help me. He's just one of them.

The air is stale. I take a deep breath, as if it's one of the last I'll ever have – which I figure it could well be. I don't know what Room Zero is, but it doesn't sound like somewhere I want to be. I wish I had something to fight back with. I wonder, suddenly, if Malions have red blood as well as red skin. Should I make a run for it now? What have I got to lose?

I do it. I run.

'Stop!' Torrin yells.

The corridor is long, too long, but I'm free of them and almost at the corner when something wraps around my ankle and I go down, my arms and chin slapping into the hard floor. I look back. A long gold rope is shimmering across the ground with a hook clasping my ankle.

Jaxz grips the other end, grinning.

And then I'm being hauled back, like a fish on a hook. My skin burns as it scrapes the floor and I grapple to hold on to something. Tears stream from my eyes, from the pain, frustration and anger.

'You are wonderful,' Jaxz smiles. 'Just wonderful.'

He unclips my ankle and pulls me to my feet. Then he slams me against the wall, twisting my back, his hand clenched around my throat. I can't breathe. His tongue sweeps across my cheek. I see Torrin take a step forwards.

'I was right – you are tasty,' Jaxz hisses. 'Like . . . berries. The Arlatans will be delighted.'

I desperately try to push him away, to kick him, but I'm struggling to stay on my feet. He's squeezing my throat so hard I can barely get air through it, and I want to wipe his saliva and stench off my face. I can see a patchwork of scars covering his rough skin. Some must have been deep wounds, leaving behind raised welts. I don't dare imagine how he came by them.

A lift is shimmering on the wall beside us and he drags me in by the throat. The white light inside is so bright. I close my eyes but it doesn't stop the glare gnawing into my head. The crawling sensation is deeper this time, like my body is being invaded. To think I used to be scared of the lift at the shopping mall – what a wimp. It even played music.

My head is still spinning when we step out. A hand catches me under my elbow as I stumble forwards. Everything is hazy until my eyes gradually begin to clear. Torrin is holding me. He looks desperate to talk, to blurt something out.

I'm so scared. I try to pull away, but my resistance dissolves when I catch the look of sorrow in his eyes. Suddenly I don't want him to let go of me. I want to ask him about what he discussed with Jazx, about how I can get out of here. Does he even care? I want to hate him.

'You can go now, Torrin,' Jaxz barks.

I feel the tension in Torrin's fingers. He's trying to stay controlled and it's taking all of his strength to do so – his skin is slowly beginning to burn again. He holds my gaze for a moment, his eyes still dull amber. He looks so much like an Earth human now – flawed, and not so perfect. His hand drops from my arm and he whispers, with barely any volume, 'I'm sorry, Lola.'

I don't get a chance to reply, to ask what he's done or why. He steps away from me and back into the lift. And with him goes any hope I have of escaping back to Earth. All my plans are turning to water and slipping through my fingers. Maybe I should end this right now, I have the means. My hand touches the pot in my pocket.

All I want to do is to kill as many of these creatures –

Malions, Kal, Arlatans – as I can. Hundreds, thousands. All of them. That's the only escape route left now. I'm dead anyway.

Chapter Sixteen

It's now that I take more notice of where I am. A small red room with the lift flickering on one wall, and a black door on another. A woman comes towards us. She's older than anyone I've seen here. And she looks human. Greying hair swept into a bun, wrinkles showing her years, and blue eyes set off by a blue silk scarf. But she has a kind of glamour, too, like an old-fashioned movie star.

She smiles at me in a friendly way. It's almost kind. This isn't what I was expecting at all.

Jaxz turns to me. 'I'll leave you in the capable hands of Margaret,' he says.

I want to smile at the strangeness of it all. Is her name really Margaret? It seems too normal. But my lightened mood is cut short when Jaxz grabs my face. *Please don't lick me again*, I pray.

'You do as you're told now – understand?' he hisses.

I try to nod against his firm hold. His teeth are sharp and jagged, capable of ripping through any sort of flesh. Malions must be meat-eaters. He sees me as lunch. Maybe he joins the Arlatans when they feast.

'You just be a good girl here, and you'll last . . . well, for a little while at least . . .'

'That's enough,' Margaret says. 'I don't have all day to stand and watch you two smooching.'

He gives a soft laugh, his stale breath smothering my face, then, to my relief, he leaves.

I scrub my hand back and forth across my skin, desperate to erase him. Margaret swipes a scanner across my blue wrist band and then lifts my fringe.

'Yes, I was told you might be slightly damaged,' she says. 'Body bruises too, I believe. I'll have to deal with them before you go on show. Now come,' she says, clicking her fingers as if I'm a dog. 'Do you have any cage burns from the punishment rods?'

'Two.'

'Mmm, pity. I can fade them a bit, but deep tissue damage is permanent. At least they're not on your face, I suppose.'

We go through the black door into a giant circular space. I stop. Set into the walls are hundreds of small egg-shaped rooms, each one with the end missing to reveal people within, two to a room. The rooms are stacked high and side by side, curving all around us. They look identical, richly decorated in gold and white and illuminated by soft pink lighting.

I glance behind me. Four Kal are guarding the door, ballams firmly clutched in their hands. I don't want to come into contact with one of those again. One of the Kal sends over a hovering platform similar to the one I used in cold storage, but this one is big enough for two people. I pretend I've never seen one before and Margaret shows me how to step on to it.

'This is Room Zero,' Margaret says as we start to glide upwards. 'You'll be sharing with Christina in Pod AX5.'

The prisoners here don't look near to death. Are they prisoners? They're clean, elaborately dressed, somehow glistening. There are no cages here and no Malion guards with their rods at the ready.

'What is this place?' I don't want to know but I have to ask.

Margaret takes my hand. It's a gentle, motherly action which surprises me. 'Look, my dear, you're out of those awful cages. Be thankful for that. Your quality of life in here will be much improved for a short while.' Her face is genuine, warm. She reminds me of my Aunty Pam, but with more make-up. 'It's quite a privilege actually. Not many get chosen for this, you know.'

Am I supposed to be grateful?

'Chosen for what?' I ask.

'To be a delicacy.'

'A-a delicacy?'

'As in something scrumptious and fancy to eat.' She smiles gently. 'Think of this as one of those lovely French patisseries, a shop window full of the most beautiful, mouth-watering delights.'

'I don't understand.' But what I really mean is, I don't *want* to understand.

'Arlatans adore the finer things too, my dear. They eat with their eyes, for pleasure, just like we do. A cake is always nicer when topped with icing and decorated, don't you think?'

I can't believe what she's saying. 'B-but that's barbaric,' I say, my words trembling and jamming in my throat.

Margaret just looks at me kindly.

'You have no choice, my dear. You have been chosen.'

The hovering platform stops outside a room about halfway up and set into the gleaming white wall of Room Zero. I hadn't noticed it from the ground, but a clear force field is across the opening.

With a wave of her worker's ring she lifts the force field. 'Now, in you go,' she says, as if she's sending me off for my first day at school.

I step into the pod. Soft carpet sinks beneath my feet. Two beds are either side of the room with just a narrow strip of space between them. A girl is curled up in one, fast asleep.

'Christina's been training so she's probably tired. You can introduce yourself later,' Margaret whispers.

'Training . . .'

'Yes, you'll probably be performing in a live feast. If you perform well enough you may get to come back.'

A live feast. I feel nauseous. 'I wish I was dead right now.'

'Don't say such a thing, my dear. You should never wish for death. Look . . .' she sighs, 'it may be a while before you're chosen to attend a feast. Enjoy this luxury while you can.'

'I want to go back to the cages,' I beg.

Being crammed in there with a load of sweaty prisoners was less frightening than this place. At least I won't get eaten until I'm fat enough, giving me time to figure out a new plan.

'I can't do that. Especially when Jaxz has brought you here personally.'

I try a different tack. 'Margaret, are you from Earth, like me?'

Margaret turns her head away, she seems embarrassed. 'Yes. Croydon actually.'

'Then help me, I can . . .' I consider telling her what I can do to end the war. What's in the blue pot in my pocket. If the Arlatans only knew we had a weapon.

'I can't. I don't want to get into any trouble with them.' Margaret fidgets with her scarf. 'Two years I've been here now, worked my way up. They find my caring nature amusing, but useful in this delicate environment. I'm like a mother. Funny really, I never had any children of my own. Didn't think I was the maternal type,' she laughs.

I don't plan on crying, but the tears are there anyway and decide to come. I think I'm nearing overload now. Too much stuff has happened. I can't handle it anymore.

'I have to get out of here.'

Margaret puts her arm around me and gives a comforting squeeze. 'You're a pretty girl, Lola. I don't think it will be too long before you're chosen to go to a live feast on board the Mother Ship.' She swallows nervously. 'If that happens, then there's a good chance you won't come back. You'll get your end. This ordeal will be over for you. '

I look at her, my eyes stinging. But a plan begins to take shape. The live feasts are on the Mother Ship. That has to mean a gathering of Arlatans – perhaps even important Arlatans. The ones that want to destroy everything on Earth.

'So what happens at a feast? They eat me?' I ask. But I'm thinking: *Not before I kill as many of them as I can.*

She nods. 'But that would happen even if you stayed in the cages. The ending is always the same, my dear. It's just the path you take to get there.'

She leads me through a door at the back of the pod to a small bathroom.

'There are toiletries for you in here, all new. I put them here myself when I heard I had a new arrival. All the clothes in the wardrobe on the right are yours, too.'

Margaret wipes some ointment on my bumped head and informs me it will be healed in a few hours. She tells me to do the same on all my bruises and shows me a button on the wall that I am to press if I ever need her.

'Margaret,' I say as she turns to leave.

'Yes, my dear?'

'You do realise the Arlatans are farming us? This whole thing is just one giant slaughterhouse.'

She sighs. 'My dear girl, of course I do. And there are many things here you don't want to know about, believe me.'

'Like the babies?' Suddenly my tears are replaced by anger and I don't drop my steely glare from hers.

She shakes her head. 'We might travel months, years, before finding a planet rich in a suitable food source. The Arlatans have extremely big appetites, they need a constant supply. Human meat is a favourite, so they run programmes for certain species they've . . . acquired. The ones they prefer.'

'You say "we" like you're one of them.'

'No, I'm just a worker,' she corrects.

'So not just a slaughterhouse, but a breeding farm, too. We'll fight back, you know.'

'Humans are intelligent. I'm sure some will try.'

'We will and we'll win.'

She raises her eyebrow. 'Battery farming on the ships is a last resort really. They prefer to get their food straight from the planet if possible. Apparently it's better when it's . . .'

'Free range,' I spit. 'This is sick, you do know that?'

'Is it any different to what we do to cows or sheep or chickens? Think about it. Do we ask a herd of deer their permission before we hunt them? No, we just do it. We see them as food, and that's how the Arlatans see us. They are highly evolved and have incredible technology. Humans will not win.'

'Not evolved enough to have compassion though,' I snap.

'I know how you feel, my dear. I felt the same at first. But they really do look upon other species as a means of survival. It's not personal,' she says.

'It is to me – they murdered my dad.'

'I understand why you're upset. But all they see is a planet rich in food, so they take it. It could be months or years before they find another. Wouldn't we do the same?'

'That doesn't make it right.'

Margaret's human but she's defending them. How could she? But it is different being on the other side – being one of the animals, the herd, with your choices taken away.

'Doesn't it frighten you? Make you angry?' I say quietly.

She twists her worker's ring around her finger. 'We have to accept we're no longer top of the food chain. Some would say it's nature's way.'

'Wiping out a species isn't nature's way. Making a species extinct isn't nature's way.'

'It can be. Everything has to eat, my dear. Nature is cruel, by definition. Now, no more of this silly talk. It is what it is.'

And without another word she leaves the bathroom and steps out of the pod and on to the hovering platform, leaving me alone and the force field back in place.

I look out across at the other rooms and wonder how it works. Are we displayed somehow? Someone waves at me from another pod on the third row. I wave back, but I can't even make out their features.

I sit down on the bed, the plushest bedspread I've ever felt, and grip my head in my hands. Patrick always teases me about seeing the good in everything, but I can't see one drop of good in any of this. Except I get to go to the Mother Ship.

I think about the Mother Ship. Where is it? Is it attached to this ship? If it is I risk killing Aimee, Patrick and Evie, as well as the Arlatans and that's not what I want. But we're all going to die anyway, so . . . I then remember the journey here, that silver dome-like structure we passed, like a jewel in the sky.

That must be it . . . That was the Mother Ship.

Chapter Seventeen

t's great to have a shower. I just stand there and let the water run over me, its warmth making every inch of my body tingle. I wash away the smell of the cages, the corridors, Jaxz. The soap has a funny scent, but I don't care as long as it gets the muck off.

I wash myself as best I can, trying to avoid my bruises, which are huge. The shower head is weird, it keeps moving around as if detecting where it's most needed — slightly embarrassing, even if I am on my own. It lingers under my armpits and around my feet, probably struggling to dissolve away the days of sweat and grime.

A white robe hangs from the wall. I slip it over my damp body and wrap it around me. I brush my teeth and even apply a little lip balm from the bag of stuff Margaret has given me. I look at myself in the mirror. My eyes are puffy from all the crying and my skin looks dull and blemished. I'm not sure why Jaxz said I was pretty. I look terrible.

I don't bother to cover my bruises with the ointment because I notice the bump on my head is fading fast. I don't want it to go. If I'm damaged, maybe they'll leave me alone for a while.

It's nice to be out of my school uniform. I slip the blue pot into my gown pocket. I also still have the sphere pendant which belonged to the girl in the cage. I hold it in my hands. What is it? Maybe she was just a crazy, but I mend the clasp and put it around my neck anyway.

When I go back into the bedroom the girl is sitting up in bed. She eyes me cautiously as I walk past.

'Hi,' I say softly. 'I'm Lola.'

She looks human, too. Brown eyes, similar to mine, but her hair is long, wavy and a soft, buttery blonde. 'Christina.'

'I just got here,' I say, realising that's pretty obvious.

'You're lucky then,' she groans, stretching out her legs beneath the cover. 'I've been here a month.'

'Why am I lucky?'

'Cos you don't know what's coming.' She grimaces again as she moves.

'Are you okay?' I ask. 'You look in pain.'

'I had a training session earlier and was caught off-guard, got a ballam straight in the back. It kills,' she says.

'What kind of training?'

'Basic fighting skills.'

152

'Who do we have to fight?' I ask.

She gives a soft laugh. 'Each other.'

'Oh.'

I didn't think things could get any worse, but I was wrong. I scan the room. It seems the only way out of this place is through the force field at the front – although escaping wouldn't be easy, probably impossible.

'So when were you taken?' she asks.

'Um, a few days ago.'

'Scary, isn't it?' she mumbles. 'I always thought you just died when you got sucked up by a Leech. Never imagined anything like this.'

'I think most people on Earth assume that,' I say. 'At least they do where I come from.' Mum will definitely be convinced I'm dead.

'Did you?' she asks, raising a perfectly plucked brow.

'I always thought there was more to it, but not this. This is way more than even I thought possible.'

'Sure,' she says, sliding out of the bed. 'Anyway, I need a shower. Food will be here soon, then you should get dressed. Workers come once a day to choose the treats for their masters, so we need to be ready. You'll probably be excluded from the first one. Margaret normally gives the new ones time to settle in. But they do like you to be dressed, as someone might spot you for next time,' she says, her voice hollow. 'I'd like to say don't worry, it'll be fine, but I'd be lying.' She disappears into the bathroom.

I like Christina already. If I still had a list of people to rescue, I'd add her to it. But I can't save anyone now. I feel like I'm playing a board game and losing badly. There always comes a point in the game when you know your opponent is just too far ahead, and there's no way back. Dad always said to never give up. He was wrong, but I'll take as many Arlatans as I can with me when I die.

I open the wardrobe. There's a rail of beautiful dresses, but no jeans and no T-shirts. My heart sinks. I'm not really a dress kind of person, except maybe in the summer on the beach. And they aren't dresses like these. I take one out. Sparkly bits twinkle in the pink lights.

I try to look for the plainest one I can find. Unfortunately it's bright red, but at least it's not covered in glitter. A drawer underneath has plenty of underwear; again, not really in my style, but at least it's clean. There's no privacy in the bedroom, so I wait for Christina to finish and then slip into the bathroom.

The dress fits perfectly, but I hate it. We really are just pieces of meat to them, although I now come with trimmings. I tuck the blue pot into my knickers – there really is nowhere else to hide it. Luckily it's small and slim so doesn't show through my dress. It's not ideal, or comfortable, but I can't risk leaving it lying around.

We get our food. A group of Malions deliver a bowl and a drink to everyone, and a platter of various breads. In the bowl is a kind of thick, warm porridge with pieces of fruit and orange syrup swirled in. It's nice, better than anything we got in the cages, and we even get a spoon. Christina smiles when she clocks the look of surprise on my face.

'Not bad, is it?' she says.

'It's good.'

'At the beginning of every day you'll get a menu with a list of dishes you can choose from. You should try the dish called stook, it's like a lamb casserole but it tastes amazing. I wish I knew which day was going to be my last, because I'd definitely order that as my final meal.'

Her words are flippant, like she's accepted her fate. I eat more of the porridge. The taste is wonderful, like nothing I could put a name to. Sweet and tangy. The breads are delicious, too. Some are fruity, others are spicy and they burn my tongue. But I can only eat about half of everything before my stomach starts aching. I'm full. I'm relieved, because I know I would have eaten all of it, and then that weird craving would creep up on me again. The one benefit of starving myself is it has left me with a small appetite.

I've got my original bowl from the cage. I recognise it from a small dent in the side. It makes me think of Evie, I hope she's eating. Her imagination will be working overtime. Although knowing Evie, she's probably not expecting me to return.

Christina wolfs down her food in desperate mouthfuls. I guess no one is spared the fattening-up process. Watching her makes me want to eat a little more. My stomach is full, but I need to deaden my hunger, which increases as I watch her every bite. Finally I shove the bowl on to the floor to stop myself scoffing the lot. I must have more willpower.

After we've eaten, Christina gets changed into a cream off-the-shoulder dress. Her taste is the complete opposite of mine, her dress seems to have more sequins and diamantes than it has material. But it isn't her sparkles that catch my eye and make me stare. Her shoulders, face and arms are covered in glistening gold paint, still translucent enough for her skin to show, but able to catch every beam of light and reflect it back. She catches me looking.

'You'll need this for next time. It's not an option, you have to wear it. The thicker the better, but I try and get away with just a thin layer. It makes us more tasty. Like the Arlatan version of chocolate. They go wild for it. Think of us as fancy cupcakes, party food. And the dresses are impregnated with the Arlatans' favourite spices.'

To my mere human nose, it's just a sickly whiff. I shiver. I don't want to think at all. 'Have you ever been picked?'

'Once,' she shrugs. 'The odds are good, to be honest. There is a Room Zero on every Prisoner Ship, and there are hundreds of Prisoner Ships. Did you see them all when you arrived?'

'I did.'

'So they have plenty to choose from.'

'But you got picked and you're still alive?'

'You fight, you win and you get to come back. Although, sometimes the Arlatans forget this and eat everyone anyway, so there are no guarantees. Could be worse though, we could be going straight to cold storage.'

'You know about that place?'

'Yeah, and obviously you do, too,' she smiles. 'How did you find out?'

'I um . . . overheard a conversation,' I lie, hoping my red cheeks won't give me away. I've always been a rubbish liar.

'Good ears . . . Useful,' she laughs. 'We love a bit of gossip.'

She seems quite cheery considering. Maybe that's what this place does to you – maybe that's how you cope.

'You've just got a single blue band around your wrist,' she asks.

'Yeah? Why?'

'That might be a disadvantage. Although you're still quite skinny, not carrying the few extra pounds that I am, so they may leave you to fatten up a bit first.'

'What's wrong with a single band?' I ask.

'Normally, the fewer bands, the more desirable you are, because you've spent less time in the cages. The Arlatans prefer just the single greens, or, of course, the ones that are captured at full weight who are below the age of forty – in other words, succulent meat which has spent most of its time living on the planet's surface. That meat is saved for special occasions . . . At least that's what Margaret told me once.'

'She's a happy soul.'

'She certainly is,' Christina smiles.

But maybe being desirable is good. Getting picked sooner rather than later is what I need. Why delay the inevitable?

'What's that around your neck?' Christina walks over to my bed and sits down. 'Is that what I think it is?'

'I don't know. Why what do you think it is?' I ask, cautiously.

'There was this Malion that used to bring us our food. He'd always stop and talk to me – well, brag actually. He told me once about special humans they're not allowed to take from the surface and how ridiculous he thought it was. He said they wear pendants in the shape of orbs and they belong to special groups on Earth who live in the safe zones.' She touches the pendant. 'I didn't think it was true, but . . .'

I immediately take it off and hold it in the palm of my hand. 'It's not mine. A girl in the cage had it. She kept saying she shouldn't be here, but they didn't listen to her. They ripped this from her and killed her. They obviously don't honour it.'

We look at each other, her fear matching my own.

'How can there be safe zones?' Christina says.

'I don't know, unless . . .'

'What?'

The thought in my head is so unbelievable I can hardly say it. 'What if the Arlatans have done some kind of deal with humans?' I whisper. Things are coming together in my mind, loads of bits all fighting to fit in.

'They wouldn't,' she says, shaking her head.

'But it's the only thing that makes any sense. The government, the army – they don't fight the Arlatans anymore, do they?'

It's the only reason I can think of to explain why they wanted Dad to stop work on the weapon; they don't want to hurt the Arlatans anymore. Even if I had got Dad's folder to someone, it would have been ignored. We've been complete fools.

'I think you're wrong,' Christina says, walking back to her bed. 'A few individuals may have made a safe zone of sorts, but no deals would have been done. They would have listened to that girl if that was the case.'

'You said yourself that that Malion who told you thought it was ridiculous. Maybe they choose not to listen. And how would he know about the pendants if it wasn't official?' Suddenly I feel very alone. Am I the only one left fighting? I look down at the pendant, and for the first time I look closely at the gold swirls covering the red sphere. They look familiar . . . Then it hits me. It's the same pattern as on the workers' rings. The only difference is the colour. I can't believe I didn't spot it before. This is proof, surely.

A high-pitched bell interrupts my thoughts, echoing around the chamber, so loud it grates on my nerves.

'This is it,' Christina tells me. 'Look appetising.'

Chapter Eighteen

I stand at the end of the bed. Everyone is doing the same. 'Will they know that I'm not . . . you know.'

'Sure, they'll have been told when they entered if any of us were unavailable. All pods change to white, but you'll have a red spotlight shining on you, so they can see what's new in.'

I look up at the red light bathing me. I feel as if I'm standing centre-stage. My stomach is churning, and I can't get our previous conversation out of my head. The pendant. Safe zones.

'Can I not just go and hide in the bathroom?'

She laughs. 'No, Margaret will come and find you. Stop worrying, you're safe this time round. Be grateful for that.'

All the lights go out in the pods and everyone is illuminated by the white force fields. It's like a massive shop window and we're the goods on display. I'm thankful for my solitary red beam. The black door below opens and two Malions and one human enter. They each have a large hovering platform and set off, gliding around the room.

'Who are they?' I ask.

'Chief workers usually, high-ranking. You'll notice the Arlatans use Malions a lot. They're a species who share their love for flesh, especially human flesh. So they have a mutual respect for one another, and what they need.'

'Right.' I think of Jaxz and his sharp teeth. I was right.

The workers seem to be concentrating on the opposite side, dragging three humans out on to their platforms. They glide past us, slowing, smiling but not stopping. Eventually they head for the door and out.

'Thank God,' I say, sighing with relief.

'Yay, I get to live another day,' Christina cheers sarcastically.

'What will happen to them? Are they going to a Mother Ship?'

'Maybe, or an Arlatan's private quarters. Who knows?'

'Where did you go?'

Christina slumps down on her bed and begins wiping the gold paint off her skin with a towel. 'Oooh, I got the biggy – a live feast on the Mother Ship.'

I look across at her. She seems so together and in control. 'How many Mother Ships are there?'

'Just the one, I think. It's where the Queens live and the chief Arlatans. That's where you get to see the real

161

monsters that have invaded Earth, to see them in the flesh and not just in your nightmares.'

'I have seen them. The ones that live on this Prisoner Ship, at least.' I remember how close I'd been to the one in the room – its stinking breath on me.

'Yeah well, times that by a few thousand, all in one place – the smell, the noise, the fear . . .'

'So you had to fight to survive at the feast?'

'I had to kill a girl, a friend. We'd trained together. I mean, I didn't actually deliver the fatal blow, but I may as well have. She was alive when I left her, albeit beaten badly. But by winning, I sealed her fate.'

'My God.' I cover my mouth.

'Never thought I'd be able to do it, but the human instinct to survive kicked in. It's funny, but I'd wished for death so many times in here, but when I was there, face to face with it, I would have done anything to stay alive.' Her strong mask begins to crack as her eyes fill with moisture. 'I'm not proud of what I did, Lola.'

'And I'm not judging you. You did what you had to do,' I say. 'I'm sorry.'

'Don't be. You may have to kill me one day.'

I shake my head. 'Don't say that. I couldn't.' I'd let her win anyway, my aim would be to lose. 'So what do you think of the Arlatans?'

I see her physically shudder. 'Gross – terrifying.'

'Very gross,' I agree.

'Massive, fat, ugly and slimy gross,' she says, shuddering again and pulling an expression of utter disgust. 'They'll rip you apart.'

Ripped – the word Jaxz used. 'Aren't they super-intelligent, though?'

'About all they have got going for them. But hey, I'll take stupid over intelligent any day if that's what I'm gonna get.'

I can't believe I'm actually planning to go to the Mother Ship, but with thousands of Arlatans in one place, well, I couldn't ask for more. I just need to get picked. 'So what are the live feasts exactly?'

She creeps closer to me and lowers her voice. 'They get us to fight one another in a big cage, and after that they have the losers for their lunch . . . while they're still alive, piece by piece. Apparently, the louder their victims scream the more entertained they are. They have to keep them alive for as long as possible. It's a sport.'

This is crazy. I think of my dad. What would he be saying to me right now if he were here? 'Chin up, Lola, you can do this, girl.'

But whatever I do, I have to do it before I get eaten. As soon as I'm on the Mother Ship. If I can.

I hardly sleep at all. The bed is amazing; it's the softest, cosiest bed I've ever been in. But every time I close my eyes I feel I'm being devoured by a set of massive jaws.

I long for Musket to be curled up at the bottom of my bed, making my feet toasty warm as they snuggle beneath his body. I can't believe I'll never see him again.

I finally fall asleep, but soon wake up in a puddle of sweat with my heart hammering. I sit up. It's quiet. The pink lights have been dimmed to a gentle hue and only

163

my own erratic breaths disturb the calmness of the air.

I've never felt such hopelessness in my whole life. Are humans really working with these monsters? I just wish I knew what was happening down on Earth. I'm panicking again, scared to breaking point, because I know now that whatever I achieve here will be useless. And besides, who knows if I'll even get picked to go to the Mother Ship?

I've given up thinking about Patrick and Aimee because it's too painful. My heart breaks for my dad and for Musket, and even for Torrin, the one person it shouldn't break for. I have nothing left, and then I think of tomorrow — will Jaxz come back? I lean over and press the button on the wall; a stupid idea, I know, but one born from desperation.

The wait seems to take ages. But then Margaret arrives and lowers the force field.

'What's wrong? I hope it's urgent, getting me out of bed.' She has three curlers wrapped in her grey fringe. I'm not really sure why I called her now.

'I'm not feeling well. I need more time before I—'

She doesn't even get off her platform. 'Don't you think everyone in this place feels like you do?' she snaps. 'You're here now, this is your fate, so grow up and stop your childish whimpering.'

My last chance has gone. I've lost. Margaret leaves with a final glare.

My fingers find the blue pot in my nightgown. It would be a simple suicide now, so easy. But it feels cowardly and I'd kill too many innocent people in Room Zero. Not what Dad spent months working for.

No, tomorrow will come, so will the workers and so will my suffering. If they're choosing for a live feast, I have to do my best to be chosen. Tomorrow I have to grow up.

Chapter Nineteen

I pick the red dress again. Christina teases me for not taking advantage of the full choice on offer. But I'm too nervous to even think about an alternative.

'The red high heels, too,' Christina says. 'If you have to fight then they make a great weapon.'

I take her advice and slip my feet into the shoes and try to stand without wobbling – not easy. The bump on my head has gone. I'm now in a saleable condition. Fortunately the dress is covering most of my other bruises.

Margaret stops by to suggest we both get a visit from Jayne, the hair expert. Jayne is a tiny human woman with elfin features and short red hair. She transforms my limp brown curls into some kind of twisted nest, which sits high on top of my head, with crystal charms entwined throughout. According to Jayne, the charms are a very sweet and rare delicacy, which, when eaten, cause a burst of tangy flavour to explode across an Arlatan's tongue. They go wild for it. Warped. Christina's mane resembles a swirl of buttercream icing, dotted with pink and silver ball things.

'We look weird,' I say to her, as Jayne leaves.

'It's never good when Margaret suggests extra pampering. I hope she doesn't know something we don't. Could be a Royal celebration on the Mother Ship.'

A big feast but I'm not ready. Or am I?

'I've had no training yet,' I say, suddenly panicking.

'Luck of the draw, I guess,' Christina shrugs.

She helps me finish primping, insisting I cover my lips in a red gloss to match my dress. It reminds me of a teacher at our school who always had perfect red lips. I crave for the memory of our whiteboard and my dreary classroom, of Art and then double English on a Friday afternoon. I loved Art. School feels like a million miles away right now.

I coat my skin in the gold paste. It's cold and wet as I wipe it over my face, neck and shoulders. I gain a golden glow flecked with glitter. I look at my reflection and realise I don't look like me anymore.

The bell rings; it's time. The door opens and two Malions enter. Good, not too many. I look, desperately hoping Jaxz isn't amongst them. He's not. They glide around, my heart stopping every time they pass. I'm so stressed I close my eyes. Minutes pass, every one torture.

'Lola, is that you?' a voice says.

I recognise it.

'Torrin,' I whisper.

He steps into the pod. 'I don't have much time. I'm not supposed to be here but I persuaded one of the guards.'

Christina looks puzzled.

'H-he's a . . . friend,' I say, unsure what other word to use.

She frowns. 'Workers are not friends.'

Torrin ignores her. 'Are you okay?' he says to me, his voice low.

'No . . .'

'I've been going out of my mind. I never wanted to leave you here, please believe me.' He touches my shoulder, his hand has a familiar warmth. 'You look . . .'

'I look ridiculous. Unless you're an Arlatan – then I look delicious.'

'Don't say that.'

'You should go.' The last time I saw Torrin he betrayed me. What does he want now?

'Probably, but I had to see if you were here and . . .'

'What?' I say.

'I heard Jaxz was taking a party to the Mother Ship today. One of the Queens has given birth again. I thought he might choose you, after everything he said . . .'

'No,' I say weakly. 'I haven't seen him.'

'You do know what a Mother Ship is?'

I nod. I know more than I want to.

'I have to get you out of here.'

'Torrin, just go away. It's too late now,' I say. I can't tell him I actually need to go to the Mother Ship, that it's my plan to get picked. And I don't trust a word he says anymore.

He stands in front of me, his dark hair hanging over one eye. 'I won't leave you again.'

'Like when you left me to die in that room? What's changed?'

'It wasn't like that. I had to take you there. It was a direct order and it was your punishment. But I knew Jaxz was interested in you. Getting you to Room Zero was my way of keeping you alive until I could think of a way to get you out.'

Do I believe him? But it's all too late.

'Go back to your life as a worker,' I say, tears building behind my barricades. I have to be strong; I have to do what's right – for Dad. 'I don't understand why you're here. You said you couldn't help me, that it was impossible.'

'Lola . . . there's something else I need to tell you . . .'

'Stop . . .' Christina warns under her breath.

Jaxz and at least five other Malions are hovering outside the pod.

'Well, isn't this nice?' Jazx says. 'I knew you'd come back, Torrin. I left instructions with Margaret to inform me if you ever came anywhere near this place.'

'Please,' I say. 'Don't punish him because of me.'

'I'll take my punishment, Jaxz,' Torrin says. 'Just leave Lola alone.'

Jaxz laughs. 'Hardly. We find ourselves with a celebration to attend, and Lola is going to be invited. And you, my dear.' He points to Christina, who's huddled against the wall. 'You're very appealing, too, aren't you? You come also.'

A Malion, even taller and wider than Jaxz, steps off the platform and slams Torrin across the head with a rod. Torrin falls to the ground, unconscious, blood pouring from his temple.

'Torrin!' I try to run to him, but the Malion steps in front of me and grabs my arms.

Jaxz is laughing. 'This is just what we need for the entertainment. Bring them all. I'll be on extra privileges by the end of the evening if this proves popular.'

I see Margaret as we're bundled on to the hovering platforms and into the small red room. She betrayed me, and yet she still has the gall to throw me the kindest and warmest of smiles.

But I'm on my way to the Mother Ship. It's really happening.

When we reach the docking bay at the top of the Prisoner Ship, a large white craft is waiting for us. We board it through a heavy door and are shoved into a row of seats. There are twelve of us from Room Zero. I can't get Torrin out of my head, his motionless body as it fell to the ground and the way he was carried away, flung over a Malion's shoulder. He can't be dead. The thought tears at my heart, even though I know it shouldn't. Christina looks frightened. Maybe it's because she knows what's coming. I'm frightened, too. Jaxz sits beside me. I press myself into the back of my seat.

'You look and smell mouth-watering,' he hisses into my ear. 'The Arlatans will be most impressed with what I've found them this time. Twelve delectable treats. I'll be rewarded well.'

The gentle vibration of the engine distracts me. A shutter lifts from the row of windows running the length of the ship. It's the same shimmering glass as the tunnel that led from the Leech. Then we lift off the ground with a smooth, weightless feeling.

The craft effortlessly manoeuvres towards a large opening which leads out of the Prisoner Ship. It's high up, almost to the ceiling, and we pass through a clear barrier like the wall of a bubble covering the mouth. I don't know why, but I'm holding my breath. Then we're out. Again I see the Leeches surrounding Earth, like Saturn's rings. But this ring is destroying us, choking the life from our planet. And around us are hundreds of Prisoner Ships, clumped together like an asteroid field, grey and imposing – humans trapped inside every one of them. I wish we could all fly home right now.

'Wanting to escape?' Jaxz leans closer. 'That doesn't happen . . . ever.'

I hold my breath, defending my lungs against his stench. I wonder what he'd say if he knew the truth, that in my pocket I have the means to destroy hundreds of Arlatans – and him. What would he do? Kill me here, right now?

We travel away from our group of Prisoner Ships towards the Mother Ship . . . I was right, we're approaching the huge silver dome with its crown of black. I look back. I can see other ships zooming around, loads of them in the distance, like a busy community going about its business. Unreal – frightening. How can all this be going on and we not know about it? As I stare out of the window, I feel the ship slowing down. If I thought the Prisoner Ship was big, it's nothing compared to the Mother Ship.

Twenty Prisoner Ships could fit easily into this silver beast. There are no windows that I can see, just a highly polished dome covered in intricate black swirls and symbols. The same as the pendant, the ring – they're all connected. Our craft glides down towards a large hole in the body of the Mother Ship. We pass the smaller black vessels, which do have windows. I see people inside, workers. Some stare as we pass.

Down and down we go into darkness until we must have reached the bottom of the Mother Ship. Our landing is gentle. The door of the craft slides open and then I'm in.

The smell hits me first. Every breath of air is laced with the same syrupy aroma that seems to be on every ship, but here it is stronger. It sticks to the lining of my mouth, throat, lungs – everything.

As we walk along the huge hallways, I can see the familiar slicks of slime glistening under the lights. It's everywhere. The red and gold walls are draped in it. Tunnel entrances pepper the walls. It's pretty clear that this place is the Arlatans' home. Small black cubes whiz around us, sucking the goo from the floor and helping to make our journey less treacherous. My arm accidentally brushes against a wall and the stuff sticks to me like wallpaper paste. It makes my stomach heave.

Four Malions as well as Jaxz escort us. A rumbling

noise gets louder the further we go. It sounds like any normal rowdy party, but I know it isn't. I'm struggling to walk in these heels and to keep up with the others. The hem of my dress sweeps the floor, and I'm constantly treading on it. This isn't the kind of stuff I've had much practice at wearing, and you need practice for outfits like this.

Jaxz drops back to me. 'How's my favourite little human?'

'Fine,' I say.

I can feel his black eyes staring down at me, but I don't meet them. He places a hand on my shoulder. His coarse, calloused skin and his long claw-like nails make me wince as they dig into my golden flesh.

'I hope there'll be a bit of you left for me to taste.'

I try not to react, but I can't stand being near him. I will enjoy killing him more than anyone else. I take myself off somewhere better. Inside my head I'm with Mum and Dad. We're camping on the cliffs, overlooking the sea. I'm ten years old and it's the last holiday we ever had together. I was so happy there. My dreaming works – I feel better.

Jaxz still has his hand on my shoulder when we arrive at a silver wall. The whole thing is sparkling like glitter dust – beautiful. I've seen enough of them by now to know that this is a force field of some kind, but bigger and more intense than any of the others. Thousands of coloured gems line its outer edge and at the top, like a keystone, is a multi-coloured sphere, dancing with light and sparkle as it rotates. It's huge. It can't be real.

'They are expecting us,' Jaxz smiles.

The twelve of us are lined up in a row in front of the wall. Christina takes my hand and squeezes it. Her action says more than any words. Jaxz waves his palm and ring across the face of the wall. I hold my breath and the force field disappears.

Chapter Twenty

The noise is incredible. The roar of thousands of voices all at once, and then nothing. A silence so heavy you could reach out and touch it. I've never had so many eyes on me. I stand in the doorway, trying to take it all in. It's the most colossal arena I could imagine. A black circular floor, and around the edge, as far back as I can see, there are Arlatans – some massive, some smaller. Workers, some of them human, are running around between the giant beasts, but not all the Arlatans are on the floor. High up, there are alcoves and holes filled to bursting with more of the aliens; others are clinging to every available inch of wall space. Above us on the ceiling, yet more are crawling. It's like a cave full of bulging, slithering slugs.

'Come, meet your masters,' Jaxz says proudly, gesturing and encouraging us forwards. But my legs are disobeying. I can't move.

Christina tugs at my hand. 'Do as they ask.'

I put one foot in front of the other as if I'm learning to walk for the first time. I think if I didn't have Christina's hand to hold on to I would collapse. My bottom lip is juddering and I'm incapable of stopping it. This is a major panic attack situation. We're guided into the middle of the arena and Jaxz, with his arms outstretched, announces our arrival.

'My masters, to celebrate this great day, I have found for you the most wonderful of treats, which will entertain you as well as satisfy your taste-buds.'

The crowd go wild. We must look tiny in the giant space. Twelve humans, six girls and six boys, all huddled together, decorated and shiny.

'They're gonna want us to fight,' Christina whispers. 'That's what happened before. The least damaged at the end of the time, wins. The losers stay behind. Last time I won and got taken back to Room Zero, but sometimes they bend the rules and keep everyone back.'

I process what she's saying, but I don't want to go back. I'm here now; I may never get another chance.

But my breathing is my immediate concern. I know my heart is racing out of control, but my breathing is matching it beat for beat. I have to get on top of this, and quickly.

'Calm down,' Christina whispers, taking my arm. 'You're drawing attention to yourself.'

'C-can't, need to get some air . . .'

Jaxz is staring at me, a puzzled look on his scarred face. He marches towards me just as a cramp in my stomach makes me double over.

'Do you have some kind of problem?'

'I'm sick,' I cry.

He takes a scanner from his pocket and presses it to my temple. 'You're not sick, but merely experiencing some kind of anxiety attack. You humans seem very prone to such emotional conditions.'

I fall to my knees just as a deep rasping sound travels towards me. I look up. It's coming from one of the Arlatans, a huge creature with rolls of black and yellow flesh that wobble in time with its roar – or is it laughter? It has the smallest of hands tucked by his side and lifts one of only two fat fingers towards Jaxz.

'English speak?' a voice booms. But the voice isn't coming from the Arlatan's mouth; it's coming from a Malion standing by its side. The Arlatan's other hand is resting on the Malion's head; it seems to be using the Malion to speak through.

Jaxz nods. 'They all are.'

'Then that is what we shall use,' he says. 'Are you giving us extra entertainment, human?' the Arlatan asks, the voice deep, growling. It's definitely not the Malion's own voice; it's too powerful for that. I think it's a male.

The Arlatan looks directly at me, but I don't know whether to look at him or the one speaking his words. I opt for the Arlatan.

I shake my head at his question, my breathing easing a

little as I fight to control it. The Arlatan opens its huge mouth, showing three rows of jagged black teeth on either side. I think it's grinning at me, although it looks more like a yawn. I want to tilt my head because his mouth looks the wrong way round; I reckon his beak-like upper jaw could rip me apart in one go. It lets out a high-pitched screech before returning its mouth back to the diamond shape, which I recognise from so many of my nightmares.

I should take the pill now and wipe that stupid smile off his fat face. But I want to give Christina the chance to get out. Give her the chance to fight and win, to go back to Room Zero.

'I like you,' the Arlatan says. 'You are an amusing human.'

I guess his head is so big in order to house his brain. His three piercing red eyes are staring back at me. The one high up in the centre is large, but the two on either side of it look too small, almost lost in the numerous rolls of fat.

'She is the one?'

Jaxz nods and pulls me to my feet. I look at him confusedly. 'The one what?' I ask Jaxz.

'The main course,' he whispers. 'Let's see what you'll do, how far you'll go, when offered a little bait.'

Bait? What does he mean? I glance back at Christina. I can tell by her expression that she thinks I've just hammered the first nail into my coffin, but I reckon I'm already in it and being buried alive.

We're ushered into a line. Christina is beside me.

'What's going on?' she mutters.

'I don't know.'

The room fills with roars of excitement and then lowers to a drone of clicking and hissing sounds as the Arlatans communicate in their own tongue. What are they discussing? Maybe they're taking bets on who'll survive. The large one that spoke to me earlier glides forwards, the Malion by his side running to keep up.

I assume he's on a very large hovering platform. I can't see because his flesh hangs over the sides. I wonder if they have, or ever did have legs. No wonder they need other species to help them. I'm surprised they can do anything for themselves, they're that fat.

He glides around us. His massive bulk coated in a layer of the goo, huge dollops of it falling to the floor, joining the splats already shed from the Arlatans on the ceiling.

'The selection process this time will be different,' he informs us.

Christina shoots me a look, and I return it with the same amount of confusion. He nods to Jaxz, who walks over to one of the girls and takes her hand. He pulls a knife from his belt. The Arlatans roar and bang their arms against their flabby flesh. The girl cries out in horror as he drags the blade across her palm, sinking it deep.

The Malion who speaks the Arlatan's words catches the blood in a cup as Jaxz squeezes it out. The Malion downs it in one swig, then shakes his head. The girl is taken away.

'Too bitter,' he shouts to his master. Everyone laughs.

'What are they doing,' I say to Christina.

'This never happened before. It must be instead of a fight.'

The process is repeated with the next girl. She is kept, the next rejected. He reaches Christina and I can see her hand shaking as the blade sinks in. She screams out, her tears streaking over her golden cheeks. Blood drips to the ground; the Malion catches a few drops, tastes it and then spits it out in a crimson spray. 'No,' he shouts.

The crowd roars their disapproval. Christina looks pale and exhausted, but relieved as she's led away. But I know by her look that she's scared for me.

The crowd are chanting, and it's a chilling and deafening sound. Jaxz takes my hand, the knife sears my skin and my cry shudders down my throat as I try to silence it. I won't entertain them. Jaxz takes the cup from the Malion, who squeezes my hand so hard I have to hold my breath against the pain.

'May I have the pleasure, master?' Jaxz asks, and the Arlatan waves his consent.

Jaxz drains the cup. 'Sweet like berries indeed, as I knew it would be,' he grins. 'But then this always was just a formality for you. After all, you are the main attraction.'

My heart misses several beats; I was always going to be picked, it's all been one big game to them.

The Malion sprays my palm with a cold gel, which seals the wound but does nothing to ease the throbbing. The tasting continues down the line.

Seven are kept for what I assume is going to be the live feast – four girls, two boys and me. Only five are sent back to Room Zero. I'm glad Christina is among them. I'm glad she didn't have to fight. I'll give her time to get back, then I'll swallow the pill. My hands close around the bulge of the blue pot at the top of my leg.

The others are crying with gut-wrenching sobs. But for some reason I feel numb, like my fear has done a runner. Then, inexplicably, the two boys and two of the girls are led away to the outer perimeter of the arena, leaving me and two remaining girls huddled in the centre of the arena. Suddenly we're surrounded by a forcefield, a cage of shimmering gold bars. What's happening?

Then Jaxz leans in to me. 'Before the live feast, the entertainment. The bait. He risked his life trying to save you — what will you do to save him?'

I close my eyes.

Torrin.

My thoughts are on my future now, what little is left of it. If there's a single chance I can save Torrin then I have to take it. I can't save Patrick, Aimee or Evie or Christina, but maybe I can save him. And hopefully still get the chance to carry out Dad's plan — because if the governments have done a deal with the Arlatans, then this war was lost a long time ago.

Torrin betrayed me once, but he came back. He saved my life. I can't turn my back on him.

The Arlatan I'd seen before glides towards us. He must be in charge. He turns to his audience and places his hand on his ever-present Malion's head. 'It is time for the entertainment,' he bellows. A deep roar of excitement fills the room, then nothing, as if someone has pressed the mute button. Maybe they're all wired up together, acting like one big brain.

'This feast will be different,' he continues. 'The young

human in the red dress has made a close companion here. One of our workers.' Laughter then replaces the roars. 'We want to test this very human idea of friendship by seeing how far she will go to save him.'

Gasps ripple from Arlatan to Arlatan, and I see everyone look up. A body is being lowered into the cage from above. The mass of Arlatans hanging from the ceiling extend their necks downwards, snapping their jaws with excitement. Squeals fill the air.

As the body gets nearer I see him – Torrin. He's tied to a golden pole and he's been badly beaten, barely conscious. I run to him, an action which causes more laughter to circulate. His face is swollen and his torso is almost stripped bare, except for a few pieces of his torn shirt. His skin is shiny with sweat and smeared with blood.

'Torrin,' I cry.

He struggles against the ropes that bind him. 'Lola . . .' he chokes, spitting blood and saliva on to the floor. I know he has no plan to get us out of this one. It's down to me now.

The Arlatan starts up again. 'You,' he points to me. 'You will fight to keep this worker alive. The other two female humans will be trying to kill him. If they succeed, then they will live and you will die. But keep him alive and kill them, then you will live. And you will get the choice of either yourself or him for the live feast.' He chuckles. 'You have a chance to save him – if you get that far.'

Jaxz hands the three of us a silver ballam each. It's really heavy. One side of the head is blunt, the other is sharpened to a silver point. 'I'm looking forward to my supper,' he hisses.

The chanting has started up again and a constant drum beat is coming from somewhere. I hear singing, and notice a girl on a raised platform amongst the crowd. She's human, but the song is in a weird alien language that seems to excite the crowd even more. She stops after a minute and then there is silence again, except for the drum.

I've had no training. What if the two girls standing in front of me are experts? I feel so small, so helpless. They are both fatter than me and one is at least a foot taller. I hold the ballam in my left hand, unable to bear its weight across the cut on my right palm – and because I'm right-handed it's yet another disadvantage.

The Arlatans at the back of the arena rise up on their platforms to get a better view.

The two girls are crouching, like cats ready to pounce.

'Hey,' I say, 'this is stupid. If none of us fights, it's over.'

'Then we'll all be in the live feast,' one of the girls shouts. 'Normally they don't let anyone go after selection, but this fight is different. We have a chance of surviving it.'

They look determined. I guess I can't blame them. I'm going to die, whatever. At least they have a chance.

'Lola, t-try and untie me,' Torrin shouts. He's only bound by his arms, and by a thick rope wrapped around his chest. But I don't have time to deal with them because one of the girls leaps at him. He somehow manages to kick her away.

I dart in front of him, my arms wide as if I'm in goal, brandishing the ballam. This is insane – it's two against one. The slug-like crowd is gradually getting louder and louder, their excitement filtering through the bars. They want blood, and they don't care whose it is.

I kick off my shoes and hold one in my other hand. Two weapons must be better than one. And Christina was right, a four-inch heel is a good weapon. Unfortunately, both girls copy me and take their own shoes off. Thankfully, I seem to have the deadliest pair.

I can feel Torrin's frustration and anger radiating behind me, but I have to stay focused on the girls. He's defenceless apart from his feet, and he's in bad shape. I move forwards. One of the girls is definitely more frightened. I guess the desperate-looking one who Torrin kicked will come at me first. The trouble is, will I really be able to hit her with the ballam? But I have to, I know that. She screams like a banshee and hurls herself at me. I step back, slipping on a patch of slime, and we're both on the ground.

The Arlatans go crazy.

The other girl looks frozen to the spot, ignoring the cries from her partner to kill me or to kill him. At least they're both as terrible at this as I am.

We've both dropped our ballams and are now down to fists and flailing shoes. I turn towards Torrin. He looks so angry and he's surrounded by smoke . . . He's burning. But how? Is it another cruel twist from the Arlatans, torturing him?

I've never punched anyone in the face before, ever. But

I grab the girl's hair and whack her so hard with the shoe that she goes rolling away from me.

'Sorry,' I say, stupidly.

The other girl looks shocked but stands her ground. I hobble over to Torrin. His face is twisted in pain as smoke laps the pole. But it's not from the Arlatans, it's from him. He's burning through the ropes with his skin.

'Don't. Touch. Me,' he demands. 'I-I've never tried this . . . b-before. Look out!'

The other girl's making her move. She's dropped her shoe and has the ballam in both hands, swinging it towards me. I move away to draw her from Torrin, but I have no weapon – my ballam is lying on the floor next to my shoe. Her ballam sweeps towards me and I jump back. It misses, but she's quick and before I can compose myself it slams hard into my leg.

It's agonising and I collapse to the floor, blood pouring from my leg. I hear excited squeals from behind the bars; maybe it's the smell of blood, or they've had a whiff of my body paint. Whatever it is, I know I have to get up, or this will be it.

She turns away from me and heads towards Torrin. 'No,' I scream, pulling myself on to my good leg – but I'm not close enough. She raises the ballam again. I shut my eyes and hear the head of the weapon smash into the metal pole. But it's her who yells out, not Torrin.

Torrin has burned through his ropes and hit the girl to the ground. Now he's doubled over in pain. The crowd are going mental.

'Are you okay?' I cry.

'We have to kill them, Lola.'

'But they're defenceless.'

Torrin grabs one of the ballams and looks at the girls, but I can tell he doesn't want to do it either.

His ragged shirt is soaked, the back and front scorched black. He looks at me, his eyes bright orange – just as they were the first time I saw him.

'Drop the ballam, Torrin. We're not monsters like them,' I say softly. 'No more.'

Chapter Twenty-One

I hear the thud as the ballam hits the ground. The crowd is silent, not a whisper or a click of their tongues. But one lone growl comes from somewhere, then another. They don't like this ending. The girls both struggle to their feet. They also know the fight is over. We stand listening to their bizarre chants. The golden bars of the cage fade, and the head Arlatan glides forwards.

He waves for silence. 'Humans amaze me. Simple rules, but not followed. And as for you,' he looks at Torrin, his red eyes seeming to glare, 'I never knew your species was capable of creating such heat. Your rage was interesting to watch. We will investigate such a power. It may be of use to us.'

He addresses the crowd again. 'It seems we have eight

to feast on,' he laughs, and their cheers are back. 'Or maybe we'll free the last one standing, encourage them to put up a fight.' He beckons and the other four prisoners are dragged, sobbing, back into the arena.

'Lola, I'm so sorry,' Torrin says.

'For what?'

'For not getting you away from here.' I can hear the anger welling up inside him again.

'I should never have asked you.' I know now that I could never hate Torrin, no matter what.

Ten Arlatans glide on to the floor. They are huge, their skin thick, scaly and wet. It's hard to tell one from the other.

'Be prepared,' Torrin says. 'They'll use their minds to debilitate you. Don't ask me how, never experienced it . . . until probably now.'

'R-right,' I say, feeling like a quivering wreck. This is pure fear. I'm literally staring death in the face. I know I have the blue pot, but Torrin could still survive this. I should throw it away; avoid it accidentally going off when I get eaten. 'Torrin, I want you to be the last one standing. Survive this, for me. Please.'

'I can't, Lola, they're lying. They can say what they like, it doesn't have to be true.' He looks up to the ceiling as if searching for something. 'We aren't going to get out of this alive.'

I have no choice then. I must do it now.

Each Arlatan has one of the Kal by their side. They probably need help with practical stuff, like catching us. But I'm not going to die like that; this is my death and I want it on my terms. I tear at the gash in my dress from the ballam strike and put my hand through it to retrieve the blue pot from the leg of my knickers.

I feel calmer all of a sudden, accepting of my fate. It's surreal. I'm heartbroken that Torrin is here, but if he's going to die anyway then this is the way it should be. A quick, painless death rather than being eaten alive.

A bell rings out.

'It is time. Feast, my friends,' the Arlatan roars.

Suddenly the other prisoners are running and screaming. The Arlatans are closing in on us, with hunger in their blood-red eyes. I run too, my leg searing with pain, through a gap between two of the creatures. I don't suppose putting distance between me and Torrin is going to help much, but I have no idea how powerful the explosion will be.

A sharp stabbing shoots through my head, like a parasite burrowing its way into my skull.

'Get out of me,' I shout, collapsing to my knees, grabbing at my hair.

Another girl screams, a torturous cry for help, a sound so chilling I freeze. I look up. An Arlatan has her. Its neck extending, shooting forwards from its body, its jaw holding the girl firmly – only her lower body now visible. Another takes her leg in its mouth, the clawed lip sinking deep into the flesh of her thigh and ripping it from her body. The crowd goes nuts, Arlatans flapping their fleshy arms like demented sea lions. But the worst thing is she's still alive. I can hear her agonised shrieks from inside the Arlatan's mouth.

I close my eyes to the horrific scene and try to run away from the pain in my head, shake it from me, but when I open them I see an Arlatan moving towards me. My hand is shaking as I try to remove one of the pills from the pot, but whatever they're doing to me it's messing with my coordination.

Torrin grabs me around the waist and pulls me back. 'What's that?' he's shouting.

'Get away from me, Torrin,' I scream.

But suddenly his grip loosens; he yells out and is yanked away from me.

'Torrin!' I cry, and turn to see him dangling by his leg above the open jaws of an Arlatan. He's being held there by the extended arm of a Kal. They're loving it, playing with him like a toy. It's more than I can bear.

'Stop it,' I scream.

I get to my feet, shaking my head, trying to get my senses back. My leg has gone numb and I have to drag it as I hobble forwards. I hold up the blue pot as high as I can so they can all see it. 'You know what this is?'

I have their attention, or their curiosity at least. I have no idea what I'm doing. I just want Torrin away from there. The head Arlatan is smiling, I think — it's hard to tell with that mouth.

'And what is it?'

'Put him down and I'll tell you.'

Laughter vibrates the ground, but to my surprise Torrin is lowered. He staggers towards me, his trousers drenched in blood and slime.

'Lola, what are you doing?'

I look at him and remember what he said before, about the Arlatans telling us whatever they want to, and it not having to be true. Couldn't I do that?

Jaxz is striding towards me, fury etched into his face.

'Stay back,' I yell. He stops and I manage to tip one of the pills into my palm.

'What is this game you play with us?' the Arlatan asks through his now frightened-looking Malion.

'It's no game. This pill will blow your Mother Ship to pieces . . . and you with it,' I say, trying to sound in control when beneath I'm dissolving bit by bit. 'All I have to do is swallow it and – boom.'

'Lola.' Torrin is beside me, too close.

I step away from him, he can't stop this . . . It's too late.

The Arlatans are still silent. Are they thinking? Are they worried? Whatever they are, they're all staring at me.

Now for the bluff.

'Every human on Earth will soon have one of these; they'll all be a walking bomb. Each time you decide to take one of us we'll be able to just explode and destroy you and your ships. It's over, you've lost. Your farming days are finished. So I suggest you pack up and go home.'

I'm trembling inside, but I can feel the mood in the arena has changed.

'Who do you work for on Earth?' the head Arlatan asks.

'Professor James Hubbard,' I say proudly. 'My father.'

The Arlatan moves nearer; he still has the girl's pink dress and entrails dangling from his mouth. I look around. The other prisoners are cowering on the floor like frightened animals. I don't know if any more are missing.

'We have an agreement with your human chiefs. No more attacks on us . . . So you are working alone. A rebel.'

'Why would they do that? Why would they deal with monsters like you?' I say, knowing I have nothing to lose now – we're all dead anyway. They won't be quick enough to stop me. I have to just hope they believe me. So this weapon can be what it was always meant to be: a deterrent.

'Fear,' he growls. 'Humans will do anything to survive, pay whatever price.'

'So what's the deal then? You allow certain humans safe zones?'

A loud rumble vibrates from his throat. 'You seem to know it already. We allow a few to continue, to carry on production for us – for future visits. Now tell me, what is in that pill? You do not have the technology on Earth to develop it. And we did not detect it.'

'Oh, we have the technology. We got it from you, actually.' I hear a few murmurs from the crowd. 'Humans will never work with you. They lied if they said they would.'

'I think you tease us, pretty human – but I'm bored of you now.'

He's staring at me and he's in my head again, piercing my brain.

'I'm sorry, Torrin,' I say softly and lift the pill to my mouth, making sure everyone sees what I'm doing.

It's not easy to swallow something when your mouth and throat are so dry, but I force it down. My head clears. The Arlatan is gliding away from me, they all are. They believe me.

I sink to the ground. It'll go off any second now, as soon as the outer coating dissolves.

There's a sense of rising panic in the room. All the Arlatans are trying to leave, but it's not easy staging a mass evacuation of such huge creatures, and there are thousands of them. At least nobody wants to eat me now, that's for sure. In fact there's a large space all around me. Torrin is rooted to the spot – staring.

I'm not scared anymore. But it's taking longer than I thought it would. My heart's pounding. Beads of sweat run down my face, salty as they settle on my lips. And then everything goes black.

Chapter Twenty-Two

Am I dead? No, I'm not dead, I'm sure of it. I wouldn't be breathing if I was dead. And there is noise and confusion everywhere. The lights are out and it's pitch black. Someone has me by the arm, dragging me to my feet, but I can hardly walk.

'Come on,' he yells. It's Torrin.

Then we're running, hobbling, bashing into Arlatans and workers, but unable to see a thing, just feeling our way. I have no idea where we are, but suddenly I sense there's more space around me. The Arlatans are moving in the opposite direction.

'Listen to me.' Torrin's voice is in my ear. 'There's a lift around here — a service lift only used by the workers. They're all busy making sure the Arlatans are getting out.

The loyal workers won't leave until the Arlatans are safe. We have to be the first ones through, okay? We need a head start.'

But my mind's in bits. What's going on? Why didn't the pill work? Am I not supposed to be in a thousand pieces right now? Did Dad get it completely wrong?

'Always have a plan B,' Torrin adds. 'Patrick . . .'

'Patrick?'

'That's what I wanted to tell you, but I didn't get the chance. Like you not telling me about that fake pill of yours. It *was* him you saw in cold storage. I found him, only he doesn't work there.'

Relief whooshes through me. I don't mention the pill, which Torrin now thinks is fake. I wish I knew what on earth was going on. I feel sick at the thought that I could explode and take Torrin with me.

'He's working on one of the three Control Ships,' Torrin continues. 'They hover just above the Mother Ship.'

'The black ones?'

'Yes. I paid him a visit.'

'So you knew all this was going to happen?'

'I knew you might end up here. We worked out a plan – but we weren't sure it would happen. And we didn't realise you had a plan of your own, or that I'd be a part of the feast.'

My mind is whizzing and I feel weird, like every second could be my last. Is the pill going to go off? Or was the threat they posed to the Arlatans just a lie? No, Dad wouldn't have done that.

All the lights and power come back on. I screw up my

eyes against it, but Torrin pushes me into the lift. The pain in my leg is unbearable. A few seconds and we're out.

It looks like we're in a huge white hangar. Deserted. Alarms are going off everywhere, red lights flashing from the walls.

'Where are we?' I ask.

'At the top of the Mother Ship. Quick, in here.' Torrin opens the door to a small room with a table on one side and a bed on the other. 'People will start returning soon when they realise the threat was fake. Now sit down.' He grabs a small bottle from the table and tears at the gaping hole in my dress. He sprays my wound from the ballam strike. This will deaden the pain. Here, keep the bottle in case you need it again.'

'You think I will.'

He shrugs. 'I have no idea what's going to happen, or if any of this will work. Now put these on and wipe that paint off your skin. You're not exactly inconspicuous dressed like that. And hurry up.'

He gives me a blue worker's uniform: a shirt, trousers and white pumps. As he turns away to treat the bruises on his face and the bite on his leg, I quickly get changed. It feels good to put shoes on; I've been barefoot since the fight. I put the pendant and the blue pot in my pocket, with the last remaining pill inside.

I can't think about it now — what should have happened but didn't. I shouldn't even *be* here.

'So Patrick made the power go off?' I say. 'Won't he get into trouble?'

'He's already loaded a fault reading into the computer

mainframe to explain the power cut. They won't even question it. It's just a blip. You forget, Lola, the Arlatans have built this place around technology – they never doubt it.'

He winces as he sprays his leg.

'You okay?'

He smiles. 'I could do with something stronger, but they only stock the basics in these medical rooms.'

He keeps looking at the door.

'Is it locked?'

He nods. 'Just nervous.'

I do my best to wipe as much of the gold paint off as I can with a cloth, but it's thick and clings to my skin like glue. I take my hair down and remove every jewel I can. Torrin shoves my dress and everything else under the bed.

'What now?' I ask.

'We wait for a sign from Patrick. He knows we're in here.'

'How can Patrick have all this control?'

'You were right when you said your friend was intelligent. Not many get selected for the Control Ships, but the Arlatans saw his worth straight away. He works on one of the master computers which control everything in the fleet. Nothing is ever questioned, not if it comes from a master computer. The workers fix them if they go wrong, which isn't often. It's a simple set-up.'

But I think of the thousands of ships surrounding Earth; there is nothing simple about any of this. I rub my hand across my stomach, imagining the tiny pill somewhere inside, waiting to explode. 'You should get away from me.'

Torrin shakes his head. 'That was some stunt you pulled back there. Are you okay?'

'I don't know,' I say. 'I really don't know.'

'What was that thing you swallowed . . . Honestly?'

'It's what I said it was, but it hasn't gone off. I don't understand it.'

'What! You really believed it would blow up? You were really going to . . .' He turns away from me. 'We need to get to Patrick and get you home before you have any more crazy ideas.'

'You can get us home?' I say, my heart picking up speed.

'There are small shuttle crafts on each of the Control Ships. Patrick is hoping to authorise one of them for an Earth visit, and I'm taking you. No arguments.'

'Will they be looking for us? The Arlatans?'

'Probably. But Patrick will wipe our scans from the system. That'll buy us some time as they won't be able to find us very easily. Quite useful having a friend on a Control Ship,' he smiles.

A small amber light begins flashing on a black panel above the table.

'That's our signal. When we leave this room, there will be more people around. You need to look and act like a worker. Don't run or panic. Got it?'

'Yes,' I reply.

'Patrick is on Control Ship number one. Each has its own lift. To get to the Control Ship we use the purple lift, okay? We need to head straight for it.'

I nod again, still clutching my stomach, unable to think straight. 'Purple,' I whisper.

'The purple lift will take us from the Mother Ship to the Control Ship. But the ships are not attached, so the experience will feel a little different. It may be painful.'

'Okay,' I answer. But I don't want to think about it. I'm trembling already and just want to see Patrick.

Torrin opens the door. He was right, the place isn't deserted anymore. There are workers, at least fifty, all running in different directions. The alarms are still going off. We pass a yellow lift, its force field shimmering like gold-dust.

'Are there any Arlatans here?' I say.

'No, they don't venture up this far.'

A human worker is walking towards us. My heart pounds. I look straight ahead, not wanting to make eye contact. What if he was at the feast and he recognises us? I bet my skin still has a horrible yellow tinge from the paint. If I lower my head, will I look suspicious? This is crazy. If I look how I feel, I'm done for. The worker walks by without a word.

I swallow hard. Ahead is a purple shimmering wall.

'Torrin!'

My heart lurches. We turn to see a young male Malion smiling at us.

'Sanz,' Torrin says, casually.

'What are you doing here?' the Malion asks, looking at Torrin and then at me.

'New worker. I was just showing her around when

everything kicked off.'

Sanz nods. 'The grand tour.'

My palms are sweaty. I just want him to go away. *Please go away.*

'The incident at the feast has caused chaos,' Sanz goes on. 'Did you hear about it? We're still waiting for more information.'

'Yes,' Torrin answers, edging me nearer the lift. 'That's why I need to get on. They'll probably want all visitors to leave.'

'Of course, work to do.' Sanz waves a hand, turns his back, and suddenly I'm in the lift.

The purple light is dazzling. Torrin was right, this time the sensation is different, really painful. My organs are going to burst, I know it. When Torrin pushes me out I can hardly breathe.

'Are you all right?' he asks. 'I did warn you, these lifts are more . . . extreme.'

'So the Control Ships aren't attached to the Mother Ship?' I say, after a few seconds to recover my breath.

'They can be if they're docked, but they're not docked at the moment.'

'So I just travelled through space?' I hold a hand up. 'No, don't explain. I don't want to know.'

I look up, trying to clear the mush from my brain. The Control Ship is white inside. Tall curved walls sweep away in front of me, studded with rows and rows of white doors. Round and round they stretch, like a spiral, and I wonder what could be in the centre.

'Come on,' Torrin urges.

We walk past door after door, each with a strange black symbol at the top. The place is quiet and there is no sign of panic. Two female workers are standing by one of the doors we pass, talking. They look up, but seem unfazed by our arrival and continue with their conversation. I glimpse a flash of their orange eyes. They're the same species as Torrin. Workers are ahead of us too, entering and exiting rooms. All too busy to question why we're here.

'I thought that Malion had rumbled us,' I say.

'Sanz? He used to work with me on a Prisoner Ship until they moved him. The Arlatans obviously haven't put our details out yet, but when they do . . .'

'Sanz'll say he saw us.'

'So we need to get out of here fast.'

This ship feels strange and cold. A weird noise is humming through the walls, like they're alive. Is this the heart of the Arlatans' world? I shiver. This place gives me the creeps.

We stop outside one of the doors and Torrin gives it a gentle tap.

When it opens, I see Patrick standing on the other side, beaming back at me.

He hasn't changed one bit. I know it's only been a few days since we spoke, but I thought being a worker might have altered him. I'm relieved to see that he's still the same — even his glasses are at their usual crooked angle. He picks me up and spins me round. I've never hugged Patrick so hard, but now it feels so right. I owe him my life.

'You're all right,' he says. 'Although you look a bit rough, Torrin.' He puts me down and ushers us inside the room.

'I'll look better in a few hours,' Torrin answers. 'But thank you for what you did,' he adds. 'Your timing was perfect. Lola here was . . .'

'Was terrified,' I say, throwing Torrin a look, hoping he can read it as, *Please don't tell Patrick about the pill. I'm not ready for a lecture . . .*

'That was luck more than judgement. I knew the live feast event had started, but didn't know who was involved. The scans were slow coming through.' Patrick looks at me seriously. 'And I already know what you did, Lola. We need to talk.'

'Later,' I sigh.

He frowns. 'Okay, later. Still can't believe you two made it out of there alive, and that the power cut actually worked.'

'I know. It was chaos for a while, but I think that helped,' Torrin says.

'I was desperately trying to look for you, Lola,' Patrick says, 'and then Torrin turns up and tells me you might be part of the live feast.'

'Never a dull moment,' I smile.

I look round the small control room. It's crammed from floor to ceiling with computers. Flashing panels of strange data. Large spinning circles of colour, with ribbons of light feeding into them from all corners of the room. It looks dead complicated. 'How have you learned about all this stuff in just a few days?'

'The Arlatans injected the info into me. They put this implant into my brain.'

'It'll be the same as mine,' Torrin says.

'Did it hurt?'

Patrick smiles. 'No, I'm fine. It's awesome, actually. I just kinda know stuff without having to learn it. This place could be pretty cool if it wasn't for the eating humans thing.'

'You are coming home though, aren't you?'

'Yeah. Who else will annoy you if I don't?'

I'm relieved, because this place could be Patrick's idea of heaven.

'Did you know about the safe zones?' I ask him. He frowns, so I take that as a no. 'Did you, Torrin?'

'No, I didn't. I'm probably not ranked highly enough to be given that sort of information.'

'I wonder how many workers do know,' I say.

'It doesn't matter now. What does matter is getting out of here,' Torrin says. 'Is there a shuttle ready?' he asks Patrick.

'Yep, docking bay one.'

'So that's it, we just fly home?' I say.

'That's the plan,' Torrin says.

'But we can't. We can't just leave without Aimee.'

Torrin shakes his head. 'There's nothing more we can do. I'm getting you home.'

I look at Patrick. 'We can't leave her here — to those monsters.'

I hold Patrick with my gaze. He sighs. 'She's right. We came here together so we leave together.'

'What?' Torrin turns away from us, his hands gripping the back of his neck. 'You're not serious?'

'We could fly the shuttle to the Prisoner Ship, and Torrin, you could get Aimee from the cage,' Patrick says.

But I'm not listening to either of them, because someone else is in my head – the little boy from the group of newbies. If I leave, I'm betraying them, all of them. Evie, Christina, him . . .

'Stop.' I take a breath. 'I want to take more home. Not just Aimee, but the whole Prisoner Ship.'

Chapter
Twenty-Three

'W-what do you mean?' Torrin stammers, looking across at Patrick for support. 'We can't!'

'I'm not leaving them . . .' I say. 'Any of them.'

Patrick and Torrin don't say a word. Is my idea really as insane as it sounds? When it's inside my head it seems perfectly possible but now I'm not so sure.

'No, Lola. That's the craziest idea you've ever had, and you've had a few recently,' Torrin says.

'Patrick, you have so much control – surely there's a way. Can't we just fly the whole ship to Earth?' I say.

'I don't know,' he answers. 'I'd need time to think.'

'Please, Torrin,' I beg. I'm determined not to let that little boy or anyone else down.

Torrin's eyes are flaming the deepest orange. I'm not sure if it's with anger or disbelief. 'Lola, you've done one stupid thing today, don't do another. We nearly died and now we've been given a second chance. We can get out of here right now. Are you willing to tempt fate again?'

'But I have to take the risk, Torrin. I'm sorry. You don't have to help me. Patrick will . . . Won't you?'

'I'll try, but . . .'

The room falls silent except for the whir and bleeps of the machines.

'Guys, there might be a way,' Patrick says, and I'm so grateful I have to restrain myself from hugging him. 'We'll have to act fast though. Because I'm new the Arlatans have ordered a guard to keep an eye on me. He'll be back any minute. I thought we'd be gone by now.'

'I'll deal with the guard,' Torrin says. 'Tell me your idea.'

'Use their technology against them,' Patrick says. 'They scan everything, don't they? What if the scans say the cages are empty?'

'The Arlatans would probably believe it,' Torrin says. 'I think.'

'I don't get it. Why would the scans say the cages were empty?' I ask.

'I could alter them from here,' Patrick answers. 'For example, if you needed the prisoners to disappear and pretend the ship was empty.'

'What do you mean?' I frown, feeling out of the loop.

'The workers can see the cages — they'll know they're not empty. I don't get it.'

'She's right. The workers will be a problem,' Patrick sighs. 'That's when my plan enters into the "I'm not so sure and this is probably a bad idea" phase.'

Torrin paces the room — four steps back and forth is all the space allows. 'Maybe not. What about a cooling water pick-up?'

Patrick nods, his face clearing. 'Now there's an idea.'

'Cooling waters?' I say. 'What are you guys talking about?'

Torrin turns to me. 'Sometimes the Prisoner Ships go to the planet surface to refill their water supply from freshwater lakes. We could alter the scans to show our Ship was due for a visit. They're always evacuated for this job with maybe just one worker left on board. Prisoner Ships cannot fly by themselves because there's no cockpit, so the Control Ship would have to guide it down on autopilot. If we could pretend we've evacuated the prisoners . . .'

'Without actually evacuating . . .' I finish.

He nods.

Suddenly my crazy idea isn't looking quite so crazy. I knew it'd be possible. Even Torrin has an upbeat tone to his voice.

'So it could work?' I say.

'But how will we convince the workers?' Patrick says, pulling me back to practicalities. 'Like Lola said, surely they'd know that the prisoners were still on board.'

'It'll be risky,' Torrin nods, pacing faster. 'And a lot will rely on the workers doing their jobs and not asking too many questions. But if we can get them all to assume that someone else is taking care of things then it should be okay. I guess we could always tell them that a team from another ship is overseeing the evacuation. If the orders come from the Control Ship they won't question it, I'm sure. Well, pretty sure, anyway.'

I now have that butterfly sensation in the pit of my stomach. An awful lot seems to be riding on luck. But it might just work.

'I could fiddle the numbers,' Patrick says. 'There's so much data and so many ships, I really don't think they'd notice. I'll add prisoner numbers to other ships, so the overall headcount would be the same. Allocate the workers to other locations. I have access to all areas.' He smiles. 'The Arlatans are *way* too trusting.'

'They rely on people's fear to ensure they're obeyed. No worker has ever betrayed an Arlatan, they wouldn't even think it a possibility,' Torrin says. 'That's why they never found that pill on you when you were scanned. It was made of a substance they didn't think was dangerous because it came from them. They wouldn't think humans capable of developing a weapon from it. Their arrogance will be their downfall.'

'Will they suspect anything when the ship doesn't return?' I ask.

'We could crash it? Major mechanical failure? That might cover our tracks for a while.' Torrin shrugs, looking to Patrick.

'Possible. I mean we'll be sussed at some point anyway,

when they re-scan, but we'll be home and dry by then, so who cares?'

'Exactly, we'll all be home,' I sigh. The rest doesn't seem worth getting hung up about. We know this escape isn't going to solve anything; the raids will carry on and humans will still get taken. But we'll be home with a crate full of knowledge to use against the Arlatans.

Seconds later our planning is interrupted. The door opens and a worker walks in. A human and, I'm guessing, Patrick's guard. He's tall and skinny, with short greying hair. A punishment rod dangles from his belt. We all stare at each other for a moment, the guard looking dumb-struck.

'What are you all doing in here?' he asks. 'No unauth-orised workers are allowed . . . What . . .?'

Torrin grabs the guard's arm and twists it behind his back, slamming him into the wall. 'Rope,' he yells.

They struggle, the guard trying to push Torrin away. Patrick throws me a length of gold rope and we both wrap it around the guard's ankles. It takes all our strength to hold him. Patrick takes a bash in the face before Torrin ties the guard's arms and gags him.

'I'm sorry,' I say as we hide him behind a computer bank in the corner. He looks furious but is unable to speak or move.

There is no going back now. I sit on the floor away from the guard's watchful eye. Torrin and Patrick talk technical stuff. One minute I think it's going to be dead easy, the next I'm terrified that we're not even making it halfway to Earth before being blasted from the sky by an

Arlatan missile.

But time is ticking.

Torrin comes over and sits beside me. 'Patrick is going to start tampering with the data and set the plan in motion. Not long now. Then you and he will take a shuttle to the Prisoner Ship. I'll stay here and guide you down to Earth. Patrick will book me out another shuttle so I can join you as soon as possible.'

'Will it work?'

'Honestly . . . I have no idea. It's a big gamble.'

'You're mad at me,' I say. 'For wanting to save them.'

'I just want you to be safe, Lola. But you don't make it easy, do you? Getting yourself taken, running off all the time, swallowing explosives and now wanting to hijack a ship full of prisoners. Oh, and that's without attracting the attention of the most dangerous Malion in the entire fleet and ending up in Room Zero.'

It does sound crazy when he says it like that. And he has every right to be angry.

'There was this little boy in the cages.' I press my fingers to my eyes. 'I'll never lose his face from my head if I don't try and save him. He'll haunt me.'

'I don't suppose we could just rescue the boy? Just the one extra passenger?'

'All of them.'

'Thought you'd say that.'

'I can't give up on them, like I didn't want to give up on finding Dad or my friends. Would you give up on your family?'

He looks stricken by my question. 'Some of us had no

choice,' he says.

'What do you mean?'

'It doesn't matter.' His eyes dim to a flicker.

'Were you taken by the Arlatans, too?' I say.

His lips tense, as if barricading in the words behind them. 'I was six. I lived on a planet very similar to your Earth. The Arlatans wiped out every living thing. I've been living on these ships for nine years, seen planets pillaged and species murdered. But this one is so similar to my own, from what I can remember of it. That's why I volunteer to visit the surface sometimes. It feels good to walk on the ground, to breathe in the air.'

'And your family?'

He shakes his head slowly. 'I'm not proud of the way I am, what I've done, but I'm not one of them. Please don't think I am.'

Patrick walks over. 'Okay, I've sent instructions to evacuate. It's with immediate effect, so we should get going. It'll be busy, so hopefully we can sneak back on board undetected.' He looks over to the guard. 'He'll be found when the next shift comes on in an hour. So we've got until then.'

I get to my feet. I'm so scared. This is my crazy idea and it will be my fault if anything happens to them. We could have been home by now. And then a pain grips my stomach, reminding me of the one reason this won't work. The pill is still inside me.

'Lola, what's wrong?' Patrick asks.

'Nothing, I'm fine,' I say. 'What's that in your hand?'

Patrick frowns, his eyes fixed on me. He hands me a

worker's ring. 'Keep this in case you need it for the lifts, cage doors or whatever. There is a control panel on every floor of the Prisoner Ship. Use the ring if you need to access anything. I've set it for English, so it will translate any data.' He frowns again. 'Are you sure you're fine?'

'Yes.' I take the ring and slide it along my finger. I don't like the way it seems to grip my skin. 'Thanks, but . . .'

'But what?'

'I won't be coming with you.'

Chapter Twenty-Four

Patrick looks at me in shock.

'I'm not safe to be around,' I say. 'I could kill you all at any minute if Dad's pill works. I can't risk that on the Prisoner Ship. I'll stay and finish what I started. They need proof this weapon works and I could be that proof.' I look at Patrick. 'Just make sure the right people on Earth know about this, about my dad, the folder. Tell everyone who'll listen. Promise me. We need to fight back against the safe zones.'

Another pain stabs through my gut. Is this it? Is it happening?

'Do not go to the government – they've done a deal

with the Arlatans.'

I have to get away from them. I head towards the door.

'Lola, stop this.' Torrin rushes over, but I push him away.

'Patrick, you go to the Prisoner Ship. Torrin, after you've guided it down, I want you to leave, too. If you care about me at all you'll do this.' The pain eases a little and I straighten up. 'I can't risk coming with you. The Arlatans don't believe the pills are real anyway – not after my gigantic failure at the feast. They think I was bluffing, so I need to prove I wasn't, make them sit up and notice. Otherwise nothing we do on Earth will matter. I'll go back to the Mother Ship right now, because I don't think I have much time.'

Torrin throws a look of despair towards Patrick.

'Lola.' Patrick is glaring at me now. 'I can't believe you ever thought your dad expected you to do this,' he says. 'He didn't intend for you . . . for you to . . .' He shakes his head and wraps his little finger around mine, like always. 'I wasn't honest with you, mate, when I read your dad's notes. It said in his file that he never completed the weapon. It *doesn't work*. I really didn't want to tell you, didn't want you to lose faith in him. I'm so sorry, but he failed. That pill is useless.'

'No, that's not true. He told me he'd found a way to end the war . . . I've got pains in my stomach . . .'

'Probably your anxiety, stress, whatever.'

'No . . .' I say. I must fight Dad's corner, but I'm failing.

Patrick shakes his head again, his dark eyes wet but stubbornly holding on to the tears that coat them.

'He probably wanted to give you hope, something to live for. He made it up . . . He lied to you, Lola. I'm sorry.'

My head feels light. This is all wrong, but Patrick seems so calm.

'No, he wouldn't lie to me, not about this.' I can feel my throat tightening, my eyes pricking. 'So . . . so it isn't going to go off?'

Patrick sighs. 'No.'

I feel sick. Am I relieved or disappointed?

'Where's the blue pot with the other pill?' he asks.

I take it from my pocket and let Patrick carefully prise it from my fingers.

'I think we should chuck this away. It's over,' he says.

'But why did he . . .?'

'Doesn't everyone lie to the person they love to protect them?' Patrick says. 'Let's go home, Lola.'

A screen next to me starts bleeping and data whizzes across it, strange symbols and numbers flit from corner to corner. A red stream of light exits the top and coils back down to a lower machine, which begins flashing and whirring. Patrick and Torrin can't hide the horrified looks on their faces.

'The alarm's been raised,' Torrin says.

Patrick runs over to a screen behind me and begins sweeping his hands over the surface, like a conductor leading his orchestra. The sound of the alarm eventually fades.

'They've shut down all shuttle movement to Earth,' Patrick says. 'The Prisoner Ship should still be allowed – but it may not stay that way for long, so best get going.'

'Let's hope they don't suspect the Prisoner Ship, too,' Torrin says.

Patrick nods to Torrin in an odd way.

'What?' I ask, because that's a nod indicating something bad, I know it.

'I won't be able to get back to Earth,' Torrin says. 'I have to stay here and guide you home. And then I'll have no way of getting back to you, not with the shuttles out of action.'

'But you have to escape. You can't stay, you're on the run,' I say. 'Surely there's another way.'

'There's a good chance they may never allow shuttles back to Earth. I'm a worker, Lola, and I escaped from a live feast. That's unheard of. I had a feeling security would be tightened. They'll be worried about being betrayed by one of us again. They've been very trusting towards their workers, but I'm guessing that'll all change now. I'm not going to be popular.'

'I don't want to leave you.'

'Don't make this more difficult,' he says, taking my hand.

'I'll stay with you, then.'

'No,' he says. 'You and Patrick are taking Aimee home to her mother, and then you're going to live your life the best way you can.'

'But what will you do?'

'I have friends that can hide me, although it's hard to know who to trust. There'll probably be a price on my head and that'll be tempting. But Patrick's given me a new identity, new scans for my worker's ring.'

Patrick smiles. 'You're a seven-foot maintenance man now. Only scan I could get.'

I want to scream at them both.

'Patrick, I'll give you thirty minutes to get to the Prisoner Ship,' Torrin says. 'As soon as I know the evacuation is complete, I'll guide you down. We can't afford to delay any longer than that. Hopefully ship-to-ship shuttles are still allowed.'

Patrick opens the door. 'Lola,' he says. 'We need to hurry.'

'Is that it, then?' I say, in disbelief. 'My punishment for suggesting that we save the others? If we'd gone earlier this wouldn't be happening.'

'You don't know that, and you have the chance to save so many,' he says. 'Don't do this.'

Am I being as selfish as I sound?

Just as he did in cold storage, he puts his warm hands on my face. 'I won't forget you, Lola. You've taught me so much – made me remember who I really am.'

'We really need to go,' Patrick urges.

'Goodbye,' I whisper, the word almost too painful to speak.

I need to remember this – to remember him.

Chapter Twenty-Five

P atrick leads the way through the Control Ship. It helps that I'm not registering on any of the ship scans. He's done a good job of deleting me. I'm trying to walk and act like a worker, but my insides churn with terror. This plan isn't going to work, I keep thinking. If they've cancelled Earth visits, surely it's only a matter of time before we're caught?

Patrick says very little, but I can sense his fear. A beam of yellow light pulses along the ceiling.

'What was that?' I ask.

'They're doing a full scan. Searching for you.'

We hold hands and walk faster, and it isn't long before

we're on board a small shuttle and strapping ourselves in. There is no docking bay on the Control Ship, just small chutes that house one shuttle each. The cockpit is cramped, only just big enough for two. It's dark inside, lit by three rows of flashing lights and buttons in front of us. The chair and straps squeeze at my body, and once again I'm battling with my claustrophobia.

'Keep calm,' Patrick says.

I take a deep breath, relieved when the shutter slides upwards to reveal the window. We shoot forwards, through one of the clear bubble-like barriers and out into space.

'Patrick, can you really fly this thing?' I ask.

'Injected the pilot programme into my brain a few hours ago. I'm not very good though. No natural ability. Remember our go-karting trip?'

'You spent most of the session stuck in the tyre wall.'

'Exactly.'

I smile. 'Thanks, Patrick.'

'For what?'

'For being here.'

'No p-problem.' The shuttle begins to judder and I can see sweat beading on Patrick's forehead as he tries to keep it under control. 'Don't want to make people notice us, need to keep it . . . steady.' We level out. 'That's better,' he sighs.

I frantically look around, hoping we're not being followed, but it all looks strangely calm outside. I look at Earth, beautiful in spite of the ugly ring of Leeches surrounding it.

'I just want us to go home,' I whisper.

Not that my life or my home will ever be how it was, not anymore. I don't think the pain of leaving Torrin will ever go away.

'Yeah, back to our roundabout and the broken swings.'

'That'll be our first stop.' I try to smile.

I don't say any more. I can't. I have to put all my energy into getting home. To making people listen.

As we approach the Prisoner Ship we slow almost to a stop. A large white transporter vessel is leaving, followed by another and then another.

'Are the workers on those?' I say.

'Should be – this is a good sign. It means they don't suspect anything. But it only takes one person to question it, so let's keep our fingers crossed for a while longer.'

'Why would they question it?'

'No reason. Every worker has a small communication device on their belt. I sent identical messages to each of them. It's from the Control Ship, so in theory they shouldn't doubt it. But when does anything run according to plan?'

'Don't say that,' I say.

My anxiety increases as we glide past the ships and enter the docking bay. It's empty, apart from one more transporter, which is just about to leave. I can see the workers inside, but I don't look at them. What if someone recognises me? I keep my head down as we leave the shuttle. We could walk to the cages from here, but instead decide to head for the lift. It's quicker and less likely to get us seen.

Patrick checks his watch. 'We don't have long. You go and find Aimee. When the ship starts moving you can open the cage doors, not before.'

'Okay, but where are you going?'

'I need to check the autopilot is working. Then I'll open Room Zero and the other cages on the floor above.'

'Sounds like a plan,' I say. I'm shivering. 'I can't believe we're actually doing this.'

'Mental, isn't it?' He places his little finger around mine. 'Best mates forever?'

'You bet,' I say.

Patrick leaves me and I watch as he runs up the empty corridor. I head in the opposite direction, towards the cages. It's eerily quiet. The cloying smell and grey walls are familiar to me, but it's different now. A deserted ship. The only sounds are my nervous breaths and the pounding of my feet on the metal floor as I run. I hope Patrick is okay. I think he feels guilty because we left Torrin behind. But that's not his fault, it's mine. This is my stupid idea. I just hope it works.

As I enter the cage room, the misery and stench engulfs me. It feels like such a long time since I was last here, yet it's only been a couple of days. The faces behind the bars look dazed and confused. I want to let them all out, but I can't, not until we're moving and we know the evacuation is complete. But I want them all to know they're safe.

'We're going home,' I shout, unable to stop a big grin spreading across my face. They all stare at me as if I'm bonkers. 'We've taken over this Prisoner Ship and we're flying it home.'

'Is that true?' a lone voice shouts from somewhere within the throng of bodies.

'Yeah, it's true,' I answer, my eyes welling up with tears. I really want to hug them all. 'The guards and Arlatans have left the Ship – it's just us humans now.'

A ripple of sound wafts from the cages, whispers and excited mutterings. Then I hear tears and cries of relief. They believe me.

I wish I could do this for all the Prisoner Ships, but even I know that would be impossible. The Arlatans probably won't notice one ship going to the surface, but all hell would break loose if they all went.

First I run to the side of the blue cage to find Evie. She'll be so happy. I cast my eyes over the hundreds of muck-smeared faces. I see the boy who always sat next to us. He looks bewildered.

'Hey, do you remember me?'

He nods. 'Yeah, you stood on my fingers.'

'Oh, did I? Sorry.' I frown. 'The girl I was friends with – Evie. Do you remember her?'

Again he nods. 'She's dead.'

'What . . .'

'They took her body out yesterday.'

'No, no, she can't be . . . You're wrong,' I choke. I look over the mass of prisoners. She must be here. 'Evie can't be dead. She just can't be,' I say, but the boy doesn't answer.

I'm too late. I feel peculiar, weightless. I wanted to save her, to take her home. I can see her face in my mind. She was always so scared, and she didn't even know the truth.

Frustration and anger flood me. Why didn't she eat just a little bit more?

I don't want to lose anyone else. I run up the narrow stairway leading to the yellow cages above.

So many young children are staring at me, some barely school-age.

'Aimee,' I yell, tears streaming down my face.

I call for five minutes, hope fading with every unanswered yell. Then a hand tugs at my shirt. Red hair. It's her.

'Aimee,' I sob, pushing my arms through the bars and hugging her. 'I'll get you out of here soon, okay? It's so good to see you.'

She looks pale, but not ill. Her eyes still holding on to their brightness.

'I missed you, Lola. Did you find Mr Topsy and Musket?'

My heart dips. 'No, they didn't make it, Aimee. I'm sorry. And I didn't mean to leave you here all alone, but I had no choice.'

'I know,' she says. 'I'll miss Mr Topsy.'

'Yeah, I know. I'll miss Musket, too.'

There is a loud scraping sound and everything begins to vibrate. I cling to the bars.

'What's happening?' someone yells.

'Don't panic. I think it's the ship moving,' I shout back. 'We're going home.'

A united cry of relief rings out. I'm not sure what emotion I'm feeling – happy, sad, scared. They've all merged into one, and I burst into tears again.

I open every cage door with a sweep of the worker's

ring. The yellow, white and red on the top decks, and then down the stairway to open the orange, blue and finally the greens. But there is no stampede of prisoners desperate to escape. Instead, most stay inside, reluctant to leave the familiarity of the cages. Maybe they think I'm lying and if they leave they'll get punished. The ones that do venture out say little, but slump to the floor and wait – that's all we can do now.

I sit on the floor with Aimee, propped up against the bars of the blue cage. She's scared, but nothing I say will alleviate her fear as she cuddles into me.

The Prisoner Ship's movement is noisier than I expected. Like a beast that has suddenly woken up – its giant metal muscles stretching and protesting. Aimee trembles. But the pain of my own fear is lost, veiled by the pain inside my chest. I've lost too many people I care about.

We haven't gone far when an almighty bang pounds my ears and the whole ship tips violently to one side. Everyone screams, terror on their faces. They all look to me for an explanation that I can't give.

'Stay here, Aimee,' I say, giving her a quick hug. I get up and stumble towards the opposite wall.

I daren't tell them my fear – that the Arlatans have discovered our plan and are attacking the ship. Where's Patrick? He should have been back by now. I need him.

'I'm going to take a look,' I say. 'It may be nothing.'

Again the ship violently shakes and rolls the other way, as if it's reeling from a fatal blow. I try to grab hold of the bars as I stumble across the floor. The already dim lights flicker and we're thrown into darkness, before they brighten again. Aimee is crying but holding on to the bars, as others roll and fall to the ground.

I keep thinking of Torrin. They must have found him. Maybe he's fighting them off and he's lost control of our Ship. He could already be dead. And I can't do anything to help him; to make the evacuation look convincing, Torrin shut down the ship's communications, which means I can't contact him – and he can't tell me what's going on.

The ship levels out enough for me to stand upright and I race through the door into the grey corridor. As I pass the feeding room I'm reminded of its butcher's smell and its gruesome purpose.

I run, but have no idea where I'm running. Patrick said he was going to open the cages on the top floor and Room Zero. Maybe I should try there, but he could be anywhere by now. I'm getting lost in the warren of grey and I can feel a panic attack welling up inside me. There are doors, but most are locked, and those that aren't just open on to empty rooms.

'Patrick?' I call, then almost trip as the ship lurches again and I steady myself against a wall. I wait for it to settle, trying not to think what this could mean. What if we're blasted from the sky? Everyone will die because of my stupid attempt to get us home. The lifts are still on and I stand beside one. But the lights keep flickering, the power isn't stable.

'It'll be fine,' I whisper. But as I try to step into the lift, the lights in the corridor dim and the lift panel fades to almost nothing. A horrific thought occurs to me. What if

Patrick was in the lift when the power went out the first time? What would have happened to him?

I'm thinking too much, and thinking the worst. I keep walking, corridor after corridor. I turn, deciding to go back, but as I do, the lights go out completely and I'm in total darkness. I'll never find my way back now. I jump as a strip of red emergency lights stream down the centre of the ceiling; their eerie glow is oppressive. My breathing is shallow and I strain to hear anything over the torturous creaking of the ship. I loosen the collar of my shirt, trying to calm down, and squeeze my hands into fists, my nails digging into my palms. Sometimes that can snap me out of a panic.

'It'll be fine,' I tell myself. 'It'll be fine.'

I begin walking again, slowly at first and then picking up the pace. The darkness makes everything look different.

I hear something. No, I'm imagining it. The hairs on the back of my neck bristle. There it is again. It's ahead of me – I think . . . a rasping, heavy sound. Or is it behind me? No, it's definitely ahead.

I look up, scanning the black tunnel entrances, which are barely visible in the low light. I wrap my arms around my body and I slowly backtrack. *Please . . . don't let it be . . .*

The rasping is getting closer and louder. My own steps are getting bigger, but I daren't turn my back on it until . . . And then I see it. About halfway up the wall, a huge mound of flesh slithering towards me. I've seen enough of them in the last twenty-four hours to know what it is. The Prisoner Ship's resident Arlatans are still here.

'Oh God . . .' I turn and leg it back up the corridor. 'This isn't happening.'

I make a left turn, but I can hear it closing in. A pain shoots through my skull and I scream, my voice echoing around the walls. It's messing with my head again, just like they did in the arena. My legs buckle, but I pull myself up, just as another pain pounds my brain. *Keep going, keep going . . .* I take a right turn and to my horror I see a blank wall in front of me. It's a dead end.

There isn't even a door. Nothing, except a small arched alcove housing a control panel. I shove myself inside as far as I can and position myself against the panel. But I'm too exposed. The alcove isn't deep enough.

I can hear it. It's above me now, slithering across the ceiling, out of sight. My heart is hammering and I'm desperately battling the pain in my head. My tears are fighting to get out, but I have to stay alert. I can't give in to my fear. A thread of slime drips down from the top of the alcove, passing my face and pooling just inches from my feet.

I press myself back further against the control panel, its lights still faintly flashing in the darkness. My breath stutters as I scan the top of the alcove. And as if things aren't desperate enough, I see the second Arlatan oozing along the wall near the ceiling, the red glow of the lights illuminating its shiny, slimy back. I can hear its teeth gnashing in the darkness.

I was so close to going home. It could have worked, I know it could. My thoughts flick to Aimee, to Patrick to Mum. I'll never see them again.

And then it happens – the first Arlatan's disgusting head squeezes around the corner. Its huge jaw lunges towards me, stopping only inches from my face, its putrid breath like acid, making my eyes water. I cover my mouth and retreat as far back as I can. Hope flares inside me when I see that the alcove is too narrow for its big head to fit inside. It can't get at me. I stare into its scarlet, emotionless eyes.

My worker's ring vibrates. Of course, I'm protected. Relief sweeps over me. With an almighty slap the Arlatan falls to the floor. I can see the other one roiling behind it. The squeals and clicks they make are deafening.

The first one still tries to get to me, twisting its head back and forth, trying to make it fit through the small space. I think it knows who I am. Maybe it can read my thoughts. Whatever the reason, it's ignoring the ring.

'Go away, leave me alone,' I yell.

But they've got me trapped. I turn around and squeeze my eyes shut, trying to block out the image, the noise. *They'll go away, they'll go away* . . . But I know they won't.

Something pulls at my shirt. I frantically grab at the control panel as the Arlatan tries to drag me out, but the panel is smooth and there is nothing to cling to. I fall to the ground. The Arlatan releases my shirt and grabs my leg. I fight to stay in the alcove, kicking with every ounce of energy I have left, but I'm being dragged out and I can't stop it.

'Please . . . don't do this,' I yell, as if they're the slightest bit interested in talking.

The other Arlatan looks like it's laughing, its bulk

wobbling. It's a game to them, just like in the arena. They're playing with their food.

I know I'm about to die, and it's going to be either slow and agonising or very quick. I pray for the latter. I think of the others in the cage room, of Aimee. God, I hope they leave them alone.

I feel teeth grip my leg and then I'm rising into the air. Pain spirals through my body. I remember the two girls in the feeding room – one flick of the Arlatan's head and I'll be gone. Or will they rip me up first? Keep me alive for as long as possible?

I wriggle and pound its mouth with my fist, trying to free myself, but I'm getting weaker and losing the fight. Its teeth pierce my skin, sinking deep. I flop backwards, my spine arched and my arms hanging as if I'm in flight. I look up to the ceiling, disorientated. My eyes close to the nightmare and my head spins and spins. *Make it quick, please make it quick.*

But I'm not prepared for what comes next.

Chapter
Twenty-Six

The world is engulfed in a flash of light that I see even with my eyes closed. The Arlatan's teeth loosen from my leg and I crash on to the hard floor. They're both squealing and writhing, their bodies burning from the inside out. Cries of pain fill the air, a terrible sound. Their jaws are open and their eyes bulging. The sickly smell of burning skin is making me choke. They stretch up as if trying to reach for their tunnels. But then they slam into the ground, missing me by inches. I think they're dead.

But I don't understand.

My eyes try to focus on the person standing beside them – Patrick? No. He's pulling a punishment rod from each of the charred bodies. I sit up and try to shuffle backwards towards the wall.

'We meet again.' Jaxz moves with me. 'I've been looking for you.'

'You just k-killed the Arlatans . . .'

He turns to look at the two lifeless mounds, smoke still rising from their eye sockets and jaws. 'Very good, these new modified rods. More powerful than the standard issue.' He waves one in front of me before attaching them both to his belt. 'Of course, the Arlatans aren't aware I've modified them. Need to keep one step ahead, but it's nice to know they work.'

'But they're your masters.'

'What, these two lumps of blubber?' he laughs. 'These are just greedy, bottom-of-the-heap types. No, I only let the influential think they are my masters.'

'S-so what now?' I say. I can't get up – my leg is bleeding and feels heavy.

'I have to say, I'm impressed with your resilience. I've never met such a determined individual. And your performance at the feast has caused quite a stir. You've made the Arlatans look foolish, and they don't like that. There's a big reward now for your capture.'

'And I bet you can't wait to claim it.'

'I'm in no hurry. We have unfinished business,' he says, taking another step closer.

'I don't think they'll reward you for killing their own.'

Again he laughs. 'Well, I'm not going to tell them. You see, I bet these two were going to try to claim the reward for finding you, not actually eat you. No, I'll tell them I saw Torrin kill the Arlatans with my own eyes, and he will be severely punished for it, just as any worker would be if they ever dare to cross me.'

'You wouldn't. I know the truth, and I'll tell them everything when you hand me over,' I snap.

'You won't be capable of saying anything to anyone by the time I hand you over. Where is your co-conspirator, Torrin? Left you already?'

So he doesn't know about our plan, and the Ship is still moving. Maybe Torrin is safe.

'I don't know where he is,' I say.

'I'll find him later. Better that we're alone for now.'

My skin crawls. He grabs my arm and pulls me to my feet.

'Please, it hurts.' My leg is limp and soaked in blood. My white shoe stained deep red. I can't even bear to put it to the ground.

He pins me to the wall. 'They believed you at first, you know, that you'd actually swallowed a bomb,' he says. 'Trouble is, when it didn't go boom, like you said it would, they felt angry . . . cheated.'

'You mean, they wanted me to blow them up?'

'No, but you tricked them, and you don't trick an Arlatan. And then the power cut . . . Your lucky day.'

'I guess it was,' I say. At least he seems to think that was a coincidence.

He presses me harder into the wall. His breath is like rotten meat. I choke it from my lungs.

'I've no need to be careful with you now, as long as there's a piece of you left to claim my reward on. Where should I start? An arm? A leg? Which is juiciest?'

I can see the belt around his waist and the two punishment rods still glowing from their recent use. Also, a small knife. I try to grab it without him noticing, but can't reach. His nails scrape away layers of my skin. I whimper in pain.

'Louder,' he insists. 'I want you to suffer.'

'No,' I spit, warm blood trickling down my arm.

He licks the blood from my skin, and I squirm beneath him, trying desperately to get the knife from the belt. It loosens, but not enough. He bites down, ripping my flesh with his teeth. The pain is excruciating, but I'm not strong enough to push him away and with his full weight against me, I can hardly breathe. I'm going to pass out, it's too much.

I make one more frantic reach for the knife, fumbling like an infant. My fingers close over the hilt and in one determined sweep I reach up and slice it across the back of his head. He stumbles, trying to stop the flow of his blood with his hand. His blood is red, the same colour as mine – my question finally answered.

'Want to play games?' he snaps. 'You don't realise how much I like games.'

I hold the knife out shakily in front of me. But he's still too close for me to make a run for it – or a stagger for it. I'm going to have to stab him to get past but I'm not sure I can do that – not even to him.

'Get out of my way, Jaxz.'

He lowers his hand, now coated red like a scarlet glove. My blood is around his mouth and he licks it away, grinning. 'Or you'll finish me off?'

'I'm just trying to get home.'

His body shakes with horrible laughter. 'Yes, Earth. Unfortunately we're heading in the opposite direction.'

'What?'

'Did you not feel the explosion? One of the fuel tanks has blown so I've turned off the autopilot and set this ship on a one-way course for the outer regions. The ship will stop when it either hits something or runs out of fuel. It's unstable. We need to get it as far away as possible in case the other tanks explode. It happens occasionally with these old vessels. But don't look so worried. We'll take one of the shuttles. I don't intend to die here, and nor will you. That will come later.'

My head is spinning. He doesn't know this ship is full of prisoners. Would it make a difference if he did?

'Please, we have to get this ship to Earth. You don't understand, the prisoners . . . they're still here, in the cages.'

He raises his brow. 'How can that be?'

'I was . . .' But I don't have to say anymore, his expression has changed.

'So this was an elaborate escape plan. You *are* different, aren't you? A real hero. Pity you've just condemned them all to death. You're so desperate to get home. But you really have no idea what you've done, do you?'

'What do you m-mean?' I'm trying to keep a grip around the handle of the knife, but I'm getting weaker, my arm numb from the bite.

'Nowhere is safe for you now, I'm afraid. You've

angered more than just the Arlatans with your little stunt at the feast. You're wanted on Earth now too. You could have ruined their cosy deal with your silly prank. The Arlatans have sent all your details to our allies on Earth, in case we couldn't find you. You see, when you were processed, your results were stored. They tell us everything about you – your name, your DNA, even your family members.'

My blood runs cold. He's lying, he has to be.

'And now this, stealing a ship full of prisoners. They'll hunt you down, believe me. It seems everyone wants a piece of you. But I'm here first and I've waited long enough.' He takes a punishment rod from his belt and suddenly the knife I'm wielding seems useless.

I take in the scene: the two dead Arlatans, my wrecked body, and Jaxz, with blood streaming from his head. There must be a way out of this.

Jaxz snarls again. 'You're hoping Torrin will rescue you? He won't. No one can help you now.' He cocks his head. 'Or maybe someone else is helping you. Your scans have been mysteriously wiped from the main detectors. I wonder who did that? And you couldn't have organised this whole evacuation scam. To do that you'd have to know someone with special clearance.'

I think of Patrick. I don't want him getting hurt. This is my fight.

'Maybe you will tell me the name of the worker that's helped you. Or will I have to find your family and punish them instead?'

Mum. My blood is boiling now. I lunge at Jaxz, the

element of surprise my only weapon. With all my weight on my right leg, I try to plough him out of the way with my shoulder, but he grabs me by the throat and plunges me back against the wall. Pain flies through my head and spine.

But I still have the knife. And as his body weighs down on mine I sink the blade as hard as I can into his chest.

He staggers back, bent double, gulping air like a beached fish. The punishment rod clatters to the ground as he collapses in a twitching heap.

I can hardly breathe. I limp around him, trying not to look at the blood pooling on the floor. I'm nearly past when he reaches out and grabs my ankle. I trip and fall, desperately trying to shake him off, but his grip tightens. I look back at his furious face. I can still see the knife sticking out of his chest. The punishment rod is to the right of me. I swing myself over, kicking at his hand as he tries to pull me towards him.

The pain in my leg is agonising, but from somewhere I'm finding the strength to keep him at bay. I touch the rod with my fingertips, but I can't quite reach it . . . He pulls me again, but by using my elbows to dig in I crawl just a few inches more.

I grab the rod, let him pull me back and then I turn and plunge the rod deep into his side. Smoke fills the air along with his pitiful cry. His hand loosens from my ankle and I drag myself away. He isn't moving anymore.

I get up and stumble backwards until I hit a wall. I'm dazed. My head is burning and everything is going in and out of focus. I try to blink the mist from my eyes but it's no good; I'm losing it. After everything, I'm still going to die in this terrible place.

Is this it? Is this the end? No, it can't be. I've got to turn this ship around . . . I think I must pass out for a few seconds, but when I open my eyes my vision is gradually returning. I can still see Jaxz at the end of the corridor, his blood forming a thick circle on the ground beside him. The two fleshy mounds of the Arlatans loom behind him. It's a gruesome scene. A scene which should shock me, make me sick. I've killed someone, but I don't care. I'm glad he's dead.

I look at my arm, it's soaked in blood and so is my leg. I have to do something about it or I'm going to bleed to death. I rip a strip from my shirt and tie it around my leg, my fingers struggling to tie a knot. I reach into my pocket for the small bottle that Torrin gave to me in the medical room. I squirt some of the liquid over the deep gashes that are on either side of my thigh. It hurts. I hold my breath and grit my teeth against the pain, hoping not to pass out again.

The liquid is cold and seems to set over the wound like a clear skin. I do the same with the bite mark on my arm. The thought of what he was going to do to me creeps into my head. He really was going to eat me alive.

I shake my head, I've got to think. The ship is juddering again. Where the hell is Patrick? But I can't wait for him. Somehow I've got to turn the autopilot back on. I get to my feet and drag myself along the corridor towards the control panel in the alcove, trying to remember what Patrick told me about accessing data.

What do I do? I sweep my ring across a light at the top and the panel springs into life — but it's dim, maybe on half-power. At least the information is in English. I flick a finger over a diagram of the ship. A detailed plan flashes across the panel. I bite down hard on my bottom lip. I'm panicking. I don't know what to press. I might make it worse, turn off the air supply of something. A loud bang sounds from beneath my feet, vibrating through my bones. The ship rolls again and I lunge across the panel. I try to stand up straight, but the ship is leaning to one side. I look at the plan, trying to work out what is what. Another fuel tank is flashing amber, but there still seem to be two that are intact. Is that enough to get us home? *Think, Lola. Do something quick or everyone is going to die.*

I start pressing everything, trying to find the autopilot. Messages flit across the screen, complicated stuff, nothing of any sense. I see the word 'Manual' appear at the top of the screen. I press it and it disappears. Does that mean it's off? Are we back on autopilot? I've no idea, but I can't do anymore from here. I have to find Patrick — he'll know what to do.

I limp from the alcove, deciding to head back to the cages. Patrick must be there by now. The Prisoner Ship is constantly tipping and rattling like an ancient relic. What if Jaxz was right? What if it explodes? Or what if we're still heading for outer space? Lost forever. I pass the viewing room and look inside. The babies are still in their cribs. The door to the room is open. Did Patrick do that?

'Patrick,' I shout. No reply.

I try to hurry, but my progress is slow. More than once

I slump to the ground, too exhausted to go on. Minutes and minutes pass, but each time I pull myself up. I have to keep going. This part of the ship is familiar and I know my way. The lights come back on. Perhaps Patrick has been stuck on another floor since the lifts went down. I get to the cage room, hoping to see his face. Instead everyone looks at me as I stumble in. They look terrified at the sight of my bloody body.

'Lola,' Aimee cries as she runs over.

A boy from the greens helps me. 'What happened to you?' he asks. He gives me his green bowl filled to the brim with water. It's warm, but perfect across my cracked lips. I gulp it down in one go.

'There were still some enemies on board, but they've gone now,' I say handing him back his bowl. 'Have you seen Patrick?' I ask Aimee.

She shakes her head and my heart sinks.

'Where is he?' she asks.

'I don't know. He's probably stayed with the prisoners on the other floor.'

'Everything is still okay, though, yeah?' the boy asks, looking worried. 'This thing's been juddering like crazy.'

'Of course,' I say, but he doesn't look convinced. Maybe he knows I'm lying.

Aimee won't let go of my hand.

'Aimee,' I whisper. 'I need to go and find a room with a window. I need to check we're still on course.' I remember the room with the chairs where Torrin took me. It had a view.

'No, don't go again,' she cries. 'Don't leave me.'

But before I can answer, the ship starts to shake with brutal force. Screams pierce my eardrums. It feels as if the whole place is breaking up. Did I cause this by fiddling about with the control panel? I look around. Everyone is petrified.

'We're crashing!' someone shouts.

We hold on to anything we can find, the bars, the walls, each other. I close my eyes and grip Aimee tight. The noise is deafening and it goes on and on. Then we're yanked from our positions and flung across the floor.

The ship is still. No one moves.

We've landed. But where?

Chapter Twenty-Seven

'Are we home?' Aimee says.

I pull myself up, aching and hurting. I take a deep breath. 'Maybe we should go and see,' I say, trying to stop my voice from shaking.

Everyone follows as I lead them away from the cages and towards the docking bay. There are no cries of excitement, just a heavy silence of anticipation. The double doors to the left of the docking bay – that is what Torrin told me. Our exit from this prison.

Sweat breaks out across my palms as we get nearer. We could be anywhere – maybe even the moon. The fear in my stomach is making me sick.

Aimee helps me as I struggle with my leg. I keep thinking about what Jaxz said, about Earth not being safe for me anymore. Was he right? If so, when I get home who will I go to? Who will I trust? Is my family in danger? Are all the people in the safe zones mad at me? I want to go home so badly, but now it might be as dangerous as here.

The lifts are working and people from the top deck and Room Zero begin to join us. Patrick must have succeeded in getting past the Arlatans to open their prisons. It doesn't take long. People from the cages stare in disbelief at the sight of the Room Zero occupants – all shiny, clean and decorated. I keep forgetting that not everyone knows the truth about the world we've been living in.

The crowd of prisoners is huge by the time we finally get to the docking bay. I push my way to the front. My heart is pounding as I limp to the lighted panel in the centre of the door. But before I can swipe the ring across it, a hand touches my shoulder. I spin round, hoping to see Patrick. But it's the boy from the greens.

'Thank you,' he says softly. 'You saved us.'

'You're welcome,' I smile, a lump forming in my throat. I turn back to the door. I really hope Earth is behind it, or he'll be taking that back pretty quick. I sweep the ring. The doors slide down and the bright light blinds us. It hurts and we all cover our eyes. But the smell of the fresh air is amazing, unmistakable.

We're home.

We're in a field by the river. My river. My town. I really did it. I turned the autopilot back on, and Torrin is still okay, because he has guided us safely down.

A huge ramp slowly lowers and I usher people down. Most take tentative steps at first, still covering their faces from the glare. Some break into a run, collapsing and sobbing into the Earth at the base of the ramp. They grab handfuls of soil and hold it to their faces. Aimee is still by my side and we walk together, as always, her hand in mine. I can't hold back my tears anymore, none of us can.

With my leg slowing me down, I send two girls to go and find help for the babies. How will we ever find homes for them all? The field is filling up and confusion is escalating. I try to tell people to move on, to find cover. I want them away from the ship in case it's still unstable. And who knows when the Arlatans will come looking for us?

'Where can I go?' a boy asks.

'Where do you live?'

He shrugs. 'Don't know.'

It hits me. I've got everyone home, but most of them have no home to go to. Some will live miles away. I wish Patrick was here. I don't want to do this on my own. I'm desperate to talk to him, now more than ever. But he's either still on the ship or caught up in the huge crowd. I'll find him later. We're free now, we have time.

More and more people pour down the ramps. I move further away, trying to get others to do the same.

'Please, head for the trees and follow the river,' I shout. 'We need to keep out of sight.'

I look back at the grey ship. Onlookers are approaching, staring wide-eyed at the giant vessel and the hundreds of tired, dirty and disorientated humans that have just disembarked.

One man is calling, 'Isabella, Isabella.' Over and over. Is it his daughter he's looking for? His wife? Everyone will learn the truth now. There will be no more lies. I've never witnessed or felt such an abundance of relief; the air is thick with it. So many people . . . I can't help thinking of how the Arlatans see us — like a herd of cattle. And the farmers live in the safe zones, as well as in the sky. I hope they all rot. How am I ever going to tell people the horrific truth?

Aimee lets go of my hand and runs towards a little boy who's wandering around looking lost. I recognise him. 'Lola,' Aimee cries, almost dragging the boy towards me. 'This is Joe, he was in my cage. I looked after him for a little while.'

It's him. 'Joe,' I say, staring at his big blue eyes — eyes which are responsible for my decision to save all these people. 'Hello, Joe.'

'Is my mum still at home?' he says. 'I was in the garden, I wasn't allowed in the garden.'

I can't take my eyes off him. He has no idea how important he has been in all of this. 'No, not a good idea when a raid is on,' I smile. 'I think we should take you back to your mummy, don't you?'

He gives me a big assertive nod.

'Come on then, let's go.'

People are wandering off towards the town. PC Jackleson has arrived, and is trying to get everyone to the town hall — I actually think he'll need a bigger town hall.

'Please, if you follow me I'll try to get you all some assistance,' he shouts. No one is really listening. A few people are helping him. PC Jackleson hasn't noticed me yet and I keep my face hidden behind my hair as I pass. I may well be verging on the side of paranoia, but I'll never trust anyone in authority anymore.

I have to get Aimee and Joe somewhere safe. How long will it be before the Arlatans find out the prisoners are missing? We walk across the small wooden bridge arching over the river; the sound of the trickling water so intense in my ears. I've never noticed it before. I take off my shoes and enjoy the grass between my toes – a magical feeling compared to the hard metal floors on the ships. I want to savour every single part of the Earth, soak it up and lock it deep inside, never take it for granted again. I've missed it so much. And knowing it could all be snatched away again in one single raid makes it even more precious.

The walk home is weird, familiar, but different – or maybe I'm different. Aimee takes Joe home with her, and I watch as the door to her house opens and her mum screams with joy, gathering her daughter up. It will probably be a while before we find out where little Joe comes from. He doesn't know his address or even his home town. But at least his face isn't in my head anymore.

I stand at my own front door. I'm thinking about what I'll do if Mum isn't here, if a Leech has taken her in the few days I've been gone. But I have to stay positive. I hesitate, then knock and wait.

The lock turns and Mum stands in the open doorway. There's no way I can possibly imagine how she must feel.

'I'm sorry, Mum,' I cry, almost falling into her arms.

She shrieks and holds me tight, as if scared I'm going to disappear when she releases me.

'Y-you came back,' she sobs, frantically brushing my hair flat, like she did when I was little. 'I can't believe you're here. I'm dreaming. Oh, don't let me be dreaming. I-I heard someone run down the street shouting about a ship landing, but I was too scared to go out. Thought it was a trick, and they'd finally come to take us all.'

'We got away, Mum. We escaped.' I look at her, trying to take in every detail of her beautiful face. 'I never meant all that stuff I said to you. I was just angry at myself. It wasn't your fault, any of it – it was mine. You were just protecting me, I know that now.'

My words trip over themselves, desperate to get out. I never thought I'd ever have the chance to say any of this, and it feels so good to tell her the truth.

'I'm sorry too, but it's all in the past now, Lola. You're home.'

Mum takes the news about Dad as well as can be expected – she's already accepted his death. But my next statement puts the fear back into her eyes.

'Mum, I want you to pack a bag and leave this house. Go and stay with Jeff and Melanie – do they still live near the church?'

'I don't know, I think so. But why? What's going on, Lola?'

'I've messed up big time. The aliens are after me and that could mean you're in danger too. But that's not all. I found out something . . . I found out why we don't fight back anymore.'

Mum listens as I try my best to explain. The safe zones, the deal, dad's folder, the pills. I skim the horrific details of my captivity; she's not strong enough to cope with that. She shakes her head every now and then, her face showing no emotion. When I've finished we sit holding hands for a while, no words passing between us. Then she gets up, grabs a bag from beneath the stairs and packs.

I walk with her to the church, which is just a ruin now. She wants me to see someone about my injuries, but I try to explain that I can't see anyone, it's too risky. She doesn't like it, but finally stops hassling me about it. Jeff and Melanie are still alive and welcome us in. Eventually we'll need to find somewhere away from the town, but this will have to do for now.

After a while I make my excuses and leave Mum and our new home. I wander back to the common. I can see the slug-like mound of the Prisoner Ship on the other side of the river. The army hasn't turned up yet – is that a good sign or a bad one? A few people are still walking around, most of them looking completely lost. I guess they'll all find a home eventually and learn to cope with what's happened to them. Time heals, Mum always says. I don't think that will ever apply to me – I'm broken for ever.

Chapter Twenty-Eight

Standing alone, I look up at the sky, wanting to know what's happening up there and hating this feeling of helplessness. Did Torrin get away in time? What if they've captured him? What will his punishment be? The thoughts in my head are so sickening; I can't bear to think them anymore.

I look out across the common. This place holds so many memories, both happy and horrible all merging together.

'Lola,' a voice cries.

I turn. It's Christina. She looks so glamorous and out of place in her pink diamante dress. We don't speak, we just throw our arms around each other. I can feel her silent, deep sobs.

'I-I thought you were dead,' she finally says, pulling away from me.

'Me too, for a while.'

'Someone over there pointed you out and said that you organised all of this,' she says. 'Is that true? If it is then you're amazing, Lola.'

'I had help,' I reply.

'The boy that came to our pod?'

My heart sinks. 'Yes.'

'Then I was wrong to say a worker isn't a friend,' she smiles. 'So where is he now?'

'He didn't make it back.'

'I'm sorry.' She sighs. 'I have nowhere to go, no family left. I can stay with you if you don't want to be on your own?'

I nod. 'I'd like that.'

We both sit, crossed-legged, by the edge of the common. We don't talk, just stare blankly at the sky. The light fades and the sky darkens — starless because of the Arlatan shields.

'What do you think is happening up there?' Christina says. 'I wonder what they'll do when they realise we've escaped?'

I shrug. 'They'll come after us again. This was only ever going to be temporary, to buy us one more chance at freedom. But maybe when people know the truth, they'll want to fight again, like we used to.'

'Do you really think they will, Lola? Do you think

people will believe us?'

I turn to her. 'Christina, the safe zones are real. We have no choice now – we have to *make* them believe us.'

I think of Torrin. His whole existence now will be one of survival. I can't help but feel guilty at what I've done to him. I have to carry on fighting, for his sake.

A few street lights flicker on around the edge of the common, diluting the blackness. I don't want them on, I want to be able to see every detail of the night sky. I don't know why, but it makes me feel closer to him.

I'm in a trance, my eyes not blinking from the inky blackness, when Christina leaps to her feet. 'What the . . .' she shouts, pointing towards the sky. A small light is twinkling. At first I think it's a star but then I see another and another, until a bright band covers the night sky like a golden ribbon. 'Their shields are down, we can see the Leeches. Why can we see them?'

My breathing speeds up as I watch in horror. One part of the golden ring gets brighter and brighter, turning into a fireball in the sky, spreading further along the ribbon. 'Oh my God, what is that?'

Christina clasps the top of her head. 'I-I don't know, it looks like an explosion. I don't understand it. Are they under attack?'

I have a bad, almost unbearable feeling in my chest. What if they've got to Torrin and there's been some kind of fight?

A sound makes me turn. I strain my ears to hear. It's a strange noise, like something slicing, whistling through the night air.

'Get down,' Christina yells, pulling me to the ground.

A large object sweeps overhead, crashing into the grass of the common and gouging out a deep furrow. The noise of crumpling metal is deafening. I blink. Am I hallucinating? It's a Leech, grinding across the common with smoke pouring from tears in the hull!

'Whoa, that was close . . .' Christina cries.

The Leech comes to a halt just by the edge of the wood, its massive black dome burrowing into the ground. A street light casts an eerie yellow glow over its shell.

'Do you think it just fell out of the sky after the explosion?' I whisper.

'I don't know,' she answers. 'Maybe we shouldn't be standing here, maybe we should run.' I feel her tug at my arm, trying to pull me back towards the safety of the trees, but I resist.

A hatch on the side opens. I don't want to run or hide, I want to look. I don't think anything can scare me anymore. I've seen 'scary' times ten, and then some. A shadow jumps out, a black shape. My eyes strain, my brain unwilling to accept what I'm seeing, and then I almost collapse. 'Oh my God . . . It can't be.'

The shape bounds towards me.

'M-Musket!' I scream.

He leaps at me, pushing me to the ground, his tail wagging so fast he keeps losing balance. He's licking me and I'm hugging him back. He's even still wearing his red collar.

Christina looks shocked.

'It's okay,' I say breathlessly. 'He's my dog, my amazing

dog.' But I'm lost in the moment, with no thought of how this could have happened. Maybe I'm dreaming, but who cares?

An icy shiver winds through my body. I stand up as Musket continues to lick my fingers and bury his nose in my palm. Christina is smiling. I frown as I look towards the Leech. Again I try to blink away an impossible vision. This isn't happening, I can't be this lucky. I take one step and then I half-run and half-limp, ignoring the pain. I fling my arms around Torrin's neck and he swings me around and around.

'You're here! How can you be here?' I cry. His body feels warm in the cool air. Musket is jumping around us. 'I didn't think you'd be able to get back.'

'That's true,' he says, releasing me.

'And Musket? How did you . . .'

Torrin squeezes my hand. 'On my way to get the Leech I passed the ship where they take the animals. They keep the dog collars – pin them up on a board – and I thought . . . you should have something to remember him. I knew it was a small thing and long shot, too. But there was a dog matching Musket's description. He was just wandering around. They'd taken a shine to him and decided to keep him alive, so I smuggled him off. It was a risk, but I had to take it.'

I bend down and stroke Musket's silky head. 'I should have known you'd make them all fall in love with you,' I say.

Torrin takes in my blood-soaked shirt. 'Lola, you're hurt.'

'It's nothing, I'm fine. But what's going on, Torrin? It looked like an explosion up there.'

'I don't know.' His face is tight with tension. Then he gently lifts my hand, smoothing my fingers flat with his. He turns it over, places a folded piece of paper in my palm and wraps my fingers back around it. 'I didn't guide the Prisoner Ship down, Patrick did,' he says softly, yet I hear the pain in his voice.

'But that's not possible. Patrick was with me,' I say.

'He wasn't, Lola,' Torrin whispers. 'He went straight back to the Control Ship.'

I try to recall; try to remember what had happened. 'No, we got back and he wanted to check that the autopilot was working . . . or something. And then he wanted to open the cages, and he did that, I know he did that.'

'He probably did those things first, but then he left. He was determined, Lola,' Torrin says. 'He begged me to let him do this one thing for you. I tried to get him to see sense, but he wouldn't.'

'Do it for me?' I say, confused. 'Why?'

'You know why, Lola. He said you were right all along – that we have to fight back. And he said I had to be here to help you.'

'But . . .' I frown, looking at the wreckage of the Leech.

'Patrick had an idea for how to get me back. The Leeches still have clearance for Earth visits. He managed to get one booked out for me – not easy because only certain people are authorised to fly them. He had to alter the scans on my ring again, but it worked. Although they're a nightmare to fly and I didn't have time to inject the info. I'm surprised I got down at all.'

'So why didn't he come back with you?' I ask. 'Where is he?' I look over Torrin's shoulder, expecting to see Patrick waiting to make a surprise appearance. Always the joker.

But when I look back at Torrin, his eyes are almost black, with only a hint of flickering amber. 'He said it was unfinished business. Read the letter, Lola.'

I gaze down at the folded note in my hand and slowly open it. I see Patrick's untidy scribble. I swallow hard and read it.

Lola,

I guess if you're reading this then it worked. I've taken out the Control Ship and hopefully some of the Leeches around Earth. I'm sorry that I lied to you, but I had to protect you. I never really doubted your dad. But I didn't tell you the truth about what was in the folder – the one important thing about the pill. The pills have to be activated first, just a squeeze of the red tip before swallowing, to snap the seal and mix the chemicals. If it isn't activated then it will harmlessly dissolve, so don't go stressing about the one you took.

You see, I never intended for you to know about that, or for you to take one, and neither did your dad. So never feel guilty, mate. But you're right, the Arlatans do need to know that the pills work. That we have the power to fight back. So I do this for you, for your dad and for humanity. Who knows, maybe I'll get a science lab named after me. That'd be cool.

You're the strong one, Lola, always have been. The one who never gives up, the one with the determination to carry on the fight. I'd rather be up here — being an idiot — than hiding at home, doing algebra. I hope this ends the war, but if it doesn't, then make them listen, Lola. I hope you understand now why I couldn't let you go through with it — you're too important. You're special, Lola, always have been, always will be. I just wish I'd been brave enough to tell you. P xx

I look up at the sky, at the burning glow. *He took the last pill. No . . .* I wrap my arms around my body like a shield. *Not Patrick.* I put my hand over my mouth, the pain building and building inside me. Torrin holds me. This can't be happening. Oh God, will someone please stop this nightmare! I just want to scream and scream. And now suddenly I'm angry, furious with him for leaving me. 'You idiot, Patrick. How could you do this to me?'

'Ssh, don't . . .' Torrin whispers.

I didn't think a heart could break more than once, but it can. 'I won't ever see him again, will I?'

Torrin's face is full of pain. 'I should have done more to make him come back. I didn't know what he had planned, Lola, I promise. He just said he wasn't coming back, and to give you the letter. I should have read it, but it was private.'

'Patrick is stubborn, you wouldn't have changed his mind,' I say breathlessly, my insides tearing apart. 'He planned it this way.'

Why didn't I tell him how much he meant to me?

'Guys, you might want to look at this,' Christina shouts.

I stand up straight, Torrin's arm not leaving me for a second, and look up. The golden ring of light is fading.

'They're . . . leaving,' I say.

'I don't believe it,' Torrin whispers. 'It's worked . . . It's really worked.'

The three of us stand, staring up at the sky. I can see stars for the first time in years. But it doesn't feel right, any of it.

'No, they can't be leaving, they wouldn't. What have we done? What if we've made them angry and they come back. What if . . .' Panic is rising through me.

'Lola, stop . . . Don't doubt what you're seeing,' Torrin says, gripping my shoulders, shaking me back to my senses. He's smiling, relief written across his features. His eyes the brightest orange. 'Let it go. We've won. Patrick did it. You did it. You've saved so many people, Lola. You're home and you've destroyed them. They're really leaving, look . . .'

'I want to, I really do. But how can I let this go? Patrick, my dad and Evie are gone . . .' I look up at the blazing sky as more and more lights disappear. It should have been me, not Patrick. I turn away from Torrin and start to walk.

'Where are you going?' Christina shouts.

I don't turn back.

'Lola . . .' Torrin's voice follows me.

But I don't want anyone right now. Musket is running ahead. He knows exactly where I'm going.

The one place Patrick will always be. The one place I need to be . . . Our roundabout, our swings – our playground. Our haven.

Acknowledgements

To write this book, and to follow my dream, I needed time, and my amazing family gave me that. Thank you, Glen, for your constant support; Alex and Pippa, for your patience when Mum lost track of time and dinner was late; my wonderful mum and dad; Shana, for reading my early chapters; and to all my virtual friends in my writers group – you're all fab.

And, of course, the brilliant team at Chicken House for welcoming me into your family: Rachel, for your expert guidance and support; Claire, who was there at the very beginning with great advice and feedback; and Winchester writers conference, without which I would never have met the amazing Barry, who saw the potential in my work and stuck with me. Thank you all so much.

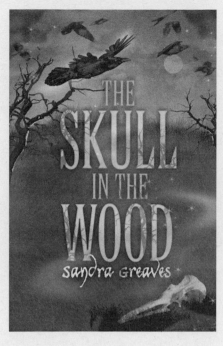